I0780015

Black Girls Day Off

Leah T. Williams

Copyright © 2025

All rights reserved.

No portion of this book may be reproduced in any form without written permission from the publisher or author, except as permitted by U.S. copyright law.

Chapter 1
The Great Escape

Maya Johnson had been practicing her sick voice for three days straight. The morning of October 10th, she stood in front of her bathroom mirror, putting the finishing touches on her signature box braids, and gave it one final run-through.

"Mom," she croaked, then cleared her throat and tried again. "Mom, I don't think I can make it to school tomorrow." She added a little cough at the end, not too dramatic, just enough to sell it.

Her phone buzzed on the counter.

Maya groaned, letting her head thump against the mirror. Leave it to their moms' decades-long friendship to almost blow up their perfectly planned skip day before it even started. She'd spent weeks researching the significance of October 11th, Black Girls Day Off – a day dedicated to the mental health and wellbeing of Black girls and women across the country. The timing was perfect: far enough from midterms that teachers wouldn't be suspicious, and with deep cultural significance that made their plan feel less like skipping and more like an act of self-care and solidarity.

Maya: new plan. everybody meet at
my locker before first period

Maya: and Destiny, please tell me you
didn't already post that TikTok about
tomorrow

Destiny: ...

Destiny: it was getting mad likes
though

Kendra: I swear you're going to get us
caught

Maya switched to her camera app, making sure her edges were laid just right. If she was going to sell this sick day, she needed to start looking peaked now. The trick, as her older sister Tiana had taught her before heading off to Howard last fall, was subtlety. "Don't come down with consumption overnight," Tiana had advised. "Plant the seeds of doubt. A missed meal here. A tired sigh there."

Maya had been sighing extra loud in AP History all week. Mrs. Reynolds, a white woman with good intentions but questionable execution, had asked twice if Maya was "feeling the burden of representation" during their unit on the Civil Rights Movement. If only she knew what Maya was actually planning.

"Maya!" Her mom's voice carried up the stairs. "You better be dressed! The bus comes in twenty minutes!"

"Coming!" Maya called back, then immediately regretted it. Sick people didn't yell. Sick people whispered and croaked. She made a mental note to start the voice fade around fourth period.

Her phone buzzed again.

> Destiny: y'all... what if we just told them the truth?

> Kendra: about black girls day off?

> Destiny: yeah like... it's kind of important for real. like civil rights and self care and stuff

Maya stared at the messages, adjusting the collar of her crisp white button-down. She'd thought about that too. Their moms would probably understand – they were always talking about the importance of taking up space, of not letting the world grind you down. But understanding wasn't the same as allowing.

> Maya: we can't risk it. what if they say no?

> Maya: this might be our only chance to do something really important

> Maya: plus I already made a whole playlist for tomorrow

> Destiny: the playlist is fire though

> Kendra: send it again, I lost it

Maya took one last look in the mirror, straightening her shoulders. Her pleated skirt and pristine Air Force 1s completed the look she'd planned perfectly – put together enough that no one would suspect she was about to pull off the biggest skip day of their lives.

Tomorrow was about more than just ditching school. It was about honoring something bigger than themselves. Maya had spent hours researching the Black-owned businesses they could visit: the bakery on Church Street, the vintage clothing store run by those twin sisters, and especially Sankofa Books, which Ms. Washington had mentioned in her African American Lit elective. The bookstore was supposed to have the best collection of Black literature in central Florida, including rare first editions.

"Maya! Bus!"

She grabbed her designer backpack (a birthday splurge her mom had surprisingly approved), already mentally rehearsing her "getting sick" timeline for the day. By sixth period, she'd be the picture of misery. She'd even convinced her lab partner to tell their chemistry teacher she looked a little green.

As she hurried down the stairs, she received one last message.

Destiny: y'all better not bail tomorrow. Black girls day off only works if we stick together

Maya: no bailouts. tomorrow we make history

Kendra: that was mad corny maya

Maya: just practice your sick voice

At dinner that night, Maya pushed her jollof rice around her plate, occasionally bringing a forkful halfway to her mouth before setting it back down with a barely audible sigh.

"You feeling okay, baby?" her mother asked, eyeing her over her reading glasses.

Maya gave what she hoped was a brave smile. "Just tired. Probably from that math test today."

Her father, a history professor at UCF who could always sense when something was amiss, studied her face. "You know, there's a bug going around. One of my TAs was out all week."

Maya tried not to look too eager at this gift. "I'm sure I'm fine," she said, coughing delicately into her elbow. "I just need a good night's sleep."

Later, as she set three separate alarms for the morning and laid out her "sick day" sweatpants (fashionable enough for their adventure but convincing as stay-home clothes), Maya felt a strange tingle at the base of her spine. The sensation wasn't nervousness exactly, more like anticipation—as if somewhere, somehow, something was waiting for her.

She fell asleep thinking of all the places in Orlando they would explore tomorrow, never suspecting that their journey would take them far beyond the city limits, to places that existed only in history books and collective memory. Places where the past wasn't really past at all, but living and breathing, waiting to be witnessed.

Chapter 2
The Portal Between Pages

T he morning of October 11th arrived with a symphony of fake coughs, exaggerated sniffles, and three mothers who were just suspicious enough to make things interesting.

"I don't feel a fever," Mrs. Johnson said, pressing the back of her hand to Maya's forehead while Maya concentrated on looking pale and pathetic. She'd pinched her cheeks in the bathroom to drain some color and had deliberately messed up her usually immaculate box braids.

"It comes and goes," Maya rasped, borrowing a line from the WebMD page on seasonal flu she'd studied last night. "And my throat feels like sandpaper."

Her mother's eyes narrowed, that familiar look that had Maya wondering if her mother had secretly been an FBI interrogator in a past life. "Mmm-hmm. Odd how you, Destiny, and Kendra all caught the same thing on the same day."

Maya's heart skipped. "Destiny and Kendra are sick too?" She hoped her surprised face was more convincing than her sick one.

Mrs. Johnson sighed, pulling her nurse's scrubs jacket from the coat rack. "Your father will be home all day grading papers. Call if you need anything."

Maya nodded weakly, pulling her comforter up to her chin.

"And Maya?" her mother paused at the bedroom door. "Whatever you three get into today, please be safe."

Before Maya could sputter a protest, her mother was gone, leaving behind only the faint scent of cocoa butter and knowing maternal wisdom.

Maya waited exactly seven minutes, counting each second, before leaping from her bed and frantically texting her friends. Her fingers flew across the screen.

Maya: My mom KNOWS. But she's letting it happen??? Meet at the bus stop in 20. Wear something cute but comfortable. We're doing this!

Across town, Destiny Turner was already three outfits deep into her options. Her bedroom floor disappeared beneath discarded clothes as she held up a vintage jean jacket with "Black Girl Magic" embroidered across the back. A gift from her grandmother, who'd taught her to sew when she was seven, it was the centerpiece around which she built her final look: high-waisted black jeans, a cropped white tee, and platform sneakers that added three inches to her already impressive height.

"You absolutely cannot leave this house," her mother was saying through the bedroom door. "You have a temperature of 97.5!"

"That's below normal, Mom!" Destiny called back, quickly snapping a mirror selfie. She hesitated before posting it to her private account, remembering Maya's warnings about leaving digital evidence.

"Exactly! Hypothermia! Back to bed!"

Destiny bit back a laugh. Her mother, a theater director at the community college, had never met a dramatic moment she didn't embrace. It was where Destiny got her own flair for performance.

"I'm going to sleep all day," Destiny replied, stuffing pillows under her comforter to create a body-sized lump. "Don't check on me. It disturbs my... healing energy."

A suspicious silence followed. Then: "There's twenty dollars in my purse. Make good choices."

Destiny grinned. Busted, but approved.

Kendra Mitchell had the easiest time of all. Her mother, a corporate attorney who practically lived at her downtown office, had simply said, "There's soup in the freezer. Don't answer the door for anyone but Ms. Johnson or Mrs. Turner." She'd barely looked up from her case files, already mentally preparing for her court appearance.

What her mother didn't know was that Kendra had spent the past three weeks working on a special art project—a hand-drawn map of historically significant Black locations in Orlando, detailed with architectural precision and decorated with quotes from local luminaries. It now rested in her leather messenger bag, alongside her sketchbook and the fancy drawing pencils her aunt had sent from New York.

At precisely 9:17 AM, the three girls converged at the bus stop two neighborhoods over from their own, far from any prying parental eyes.

"You look suspiciously healthy," Kendra observed, taking in Maya's perfectly coordinated outfit of dark jeans, crisp white sneakers, and an oversized button-down knotted at her waist.

"And you look suspiciously artistic for someone with the flu," Maya retorted, nodding at Kendra's paint-splattered overalls and the smudge of charcoal on her temple.

Destiny twirled between them, her jacket catching the morning sunlight. "And I look suspiciously fabulous."

They fell into step together, the familiar rhythm of their friendship carrying them toward the bus that would take them downtown. Their plan was simple: breakfast at Nikki's Soul Food Kitchen, shopping at Sisters' Vintage Collection, and then the centerpiece of their day—hours exploring Sankofa Books.

"You think Ms. Washington was exaggerating about this bookstore?" Destiny asked as they settled into their bus seats. "Because I'm not trying to spend my freedom day looking at dusty old books."

Kendra pulled out her map, unfolding it carefully. "It's not just any bookstore. It's one of the oldest Black-owned businesses in the city. The building used to be a meeting place for civil rights organizers in the sixties."

"And," Maya added, "they have a whole room dedicated to Zora Neale Hurston. Ms. Washington said there are letters she wrote that aren't published anywhere else."

Destiny squinted suspiciously at her friends. "Y'all are such nerds. Good thing you have me to document this historic nerd gathering." She mimed taking photos, though her phone remained tucked in her pocket after Maya's stern lecture about digital footprints.

The bus lurched forward, carrying them away from their neighborhood and into a day that stretched before them like an unwritten page. Through the windows, Orlando transformed from suburban sprawl to vibrant urban center, the city coming alive with possibilities.

Their first stop, breakfast, passed in a blur of laughter and syrup-soaked waffles. Nikki herself, a woman with silver locs and hands that had been cooking for five decades, insisted on bringing them extra biscuits "for growing minds playing hooky." They left with full stomachs and promises to return.

Sisters' Vintage yielded treasures: a pair of gold hoop earrings for Maya that the owner swore had once belonged to a background dancer in a Janet Jackson video; a 90s-era fanny pack for Destiny that she immediately strapped across her chest "like the cool kids"; and for Kendra, a set of postcards featuring Black artists from the Harlem Renaissance.

By the time they approached Sankofa Books, the afternoon sun had reached its peak, casting sharp shadows across the historic brick building. Nestled between a modern juice bar and a cell phone repair shop, the bookstore seemed to exist in its own timeline—the brick weathered to a deep russet, the windows trimmed in faded gold paint, the wooden sign hand-carved with the sankofa bird looking backward over its shoulder.

"Remember," the sign read beneath the bird, "to know where you're going, you must know where you've been."

"That's deep," Destiny said, snapping her fanny pack importantly. "You think they sell T-shirts with that on it?"

Maya rolled her eyes but couldn't suppress her smile as she pushed open the heavy wooden door. A small brass bell announced their arrival, its clear tone reverberating through air that smelled of vanilla, old paper, and something else—something indefinable that made the hair on the back of her neck stand up.

The shop appeared empty of customers, its narrow aisles formed by bookshelves that stretched from floor to ceiling. Spines of every color created a rainbow of literary history, some so old their titles had faded to illegibility, others brand new and gleaming.

"Hello?" Maya called, her voice sounding strange in the hushed atmosphere. "Anyone here?"

No answer came, but something rustled in the back corner of the store.

"We should go," Kendra whispered, suddenly gripping Maya's wrist. "Something feels weird."

"It's a bookstore, not a haunted house," Destiny said, but her usual confidence wavered as she glanced around. "Though it is giving horror movie opening scene."

Maya shook off her friends' concerns, drawn toward a section labeled "Rare Collections" in elegant gold script. There, on a stand of dark mahogany, rested a book unlike any she'd seen before. Its cover was made of what appeared to be hand-tooled leather, the title embossed rather than printed: "The Unwritten History."

"Check this out," she called to her friends, reaching for the book.

"Don't touch that," came a voice from behind them, causing all three girls to jump.

They turned to find a woman regarding them with keen interest. She wasn't old exactly, but her age was impossible to determine—she could have been forty or seventy, her smooth dark skin offering no clues, her close-cropped silver hair framing a face of timeless features. She wore a flowing caftan of geometric patterns in shades of indigo and gold.

"Sorry," Maya stammered. "We were just looking."

"No, you weren't," the woman said, her voice rich like honey over gravel. "You were about to touch. There's a difference." She moved closer, studying each of them in turn. "Shouldn't you three be in school?"

Kendra stepped forward, always the quickest with adults. "It's Black Girls Day Off, ma'am. A day for self-care and cultural affirmation."

The woman's expression remained neutral, but something flickered in her dark eyes. "Is that so?"

"Yes, ma'am," Maya added. "We wanted to visit important Black landmarks in Orlando. Ms. Washington—our literature teacher—recommended your store. She said you have original Zora Neale Hurston letters?"

At the mention of Ms. Washington, the woman's demeanor softened slightly. "Loretta sent you? Well, then." She extended a hand adorned with silver rings on every finger. "I'm Dr. Eleanor Freeman. This is my shop."

They introduced themselves, each shaking her cool, dry hand.

"So," Dr. Freeman said when the formalities concluded, "you've chosen to honor this day by seeking knowledge of your past?"

"And shopping," Destiny added. "And waffles. Well-rounded cultural experience."

To their surprise, Dr. Freeman laughed, a sound like wind chimes in a summer breeze. "Honesty. Good. That will serve you well where you're going."

"Which is... the Zora Neale Hurston collection?" Maya ventured, suddenly unsure.

Dr. Freeman's gaze returned to the book Maya had been about to touch. "No. Somewhere else entirely." She gestured to the book. "You were drawn to this for a reason. All three of you, place your hands on the cover."

They exchanged glances, a silent conversation of raised eyebrows and subtle head shakes.

"It's just a book," Dr. Freeman said, though her tone suggested it was anything but. "Either you want to learn about your history or you don't."

"We can just Google it," Destiny whispered, but Maya was already stepping forward, compelled by curiosity and something deeper—that same tingling she'd felt the night before, now spreading from her spine to her fingertips.

"Come on," she urged her friends. "What's the worst that could happen?"

Kendra sighed. "In every movie ever, those are famous last words."

Nevertheless, they joined Maya, forming a semicircle around the book.

"Together," Dr. Freeman instructed. "On the count of three. One... two... three."

Their hands descended in unison onto the leather cover. The moment skin met leather, the world around them began to shift. The bookstore seemed to stretch and warp, the shelves elongating impossibly, the ceiling receding into darkness.

"What's happening?" Destiny cried, trying to pull her hand away but finding it stuck fast to the book's surface.

"History," Dr. Freeman said simply, her voice suddenly distant, "is never just words on a page. It must be witnessed. It must be felt."

The floor beneath them seemed to dissolve, leaving them suspended in a swirling vortex of colors and fragments of sound—snatches of music, snippets of speeches, whispered conversations, and thunderous declarations.

"I can't let go!" Kendra shouted over the cacophony.

"Don't try," came Dr. Freeman's voice, though she was no longer visible. "Let the book take you where you need to go. Remember: to find your way back, you must learn what history has been trying to teach you."

And then they were falling—spinning—flying—through time and space, the book still clutched in their joined hands, until suddenly, violently, they landed on solid ground.

The smell hit them first: fried foods, cigarette smoke, and the unmistakable mustiness of a building filled with too many bodies in too small a space. Then came the sounds: a jukebox playing Sam Cooke, the clink of glasses, low murmuring conversations, occasional bursts of laughter.

Maya opened her eyes first. They were crouched in what appeared to be the back storeroom of a diner, surrounded by stacked crates and boxes of supplies. Through the partially open door, she could see a crowded restaurant where Black patrons in vintage clothing sat at tables and booths.

"Where are we?" Destiny whispered, finally able to release the book, which Maya quickly shoved into her backpack.

Kendra peered through the doorway, her artist's eye taking in details. "When," she corrected softly. "I think the question is when are we."

A calendar hanging on the storeroom wall confirmed her suspicion. February 1960.

"Oh my God," Maya breathed, understanding dawning. "We're about to witness a sit-in. We're in Greensboro."

"North Carolina?" Destiny hissed. "That's not even the same state! We need to get back!"

"I don't think we can," Kendra said, pointing to Maya's backpack where the book had been. "Look."

The backpack was empty. The book had vanished.

Outside, in the main part of the diner, someone turned up the volume on the jukebox. Through the door, they could see four young Black men in crisp shirts and ties enter, textbooks under their arms, their faces set with determination as they approached the whites-only counter.

"We can't leave now," Maya said, her heart pounding with fear and excitement. "This is history happening right in front of us."

Destiny groaned. "I knew I should have faked a sprained ankle instead."

Chapter 3
A Seat at History's Table

The storeroom door creaked as Maya pushed it open another inch, giving them a better view of the unfolding scene. The four young men had taken seats at the whites-only lunch counter, their postures straight-backed but relaxed, as if they belonged there—which, of course, they did.

"Those are the Greensboro Four," Maya whispered, her voice tinged with awe. "Joseph McNeil, Franklin McCain, Ezell Blair Jr., and David Richmond. They're freshmen at North Carolina A&T."

"How do you know all that?" Destiny asked, crouching beside her.

"Some of us pay attention in Ms. Washington's class," Maya replied, unable to tear her eyes from the scene. "This is February 1, 1960. Day one of the Greensboro sit-ins."

Kendra had already pulled out her sketchbook, her pencil moving rapidly across the page. "Look at their faces," she murmured. "They know exactly what they're doing."

The white waitress behind the counter was staring at the young men with undisguised hostility, her hands planted firmly on her hips. "We don't serve colored here," she said loudly enough for the entire diner to hear.

Maya flinched at the slur, but the young men at the counter didn't react.

"I just want to buy a coffee," one of the men—Franklin McCain, Maya thought—said calmly. "Same as anyone else."

"You need to leave," the waitress insisted.

"Actually, ma'am, we're paying customers," another of the men replied. "We'd like to be served, please."

Destiny inched closer to the door. "Why aren't they fighting back? She's being horrible."

"That's the whole point," Maya explained. "Nonviolent resistance. They're going to just sit there, not causing any trouble, until closing time. They'll come back tomorrow with more students. Within days, there will be hundreds."

A white man in a nearby booth stood up abruptly, his chair scraping loudly against the floor. "You heard the lady," he called. "We don't want your kind in here."

Other white patrons joined in, their voices rising in a chorus of hostility. The Black patrons in the diner kept their heads down, some quietly finishing their meals before slipping out the door, others watching the scene unfold with a mixture of fear and hope in their eyes.

"We should help them," Destiny said suddenly, starting to rise from their hiding place.

Kendra yanked her back down. "Are you crazy? We can't interfere. We don't know what would happen."

"But we know they're right," Destiny argued. "We can't just hide and watch."

Maya's mind raced. What had Dr. Freeman said? The book had brought them here to witness history, to learn something. But was witnessing enough? Or were they meant to participate?

Before she could decide, the storeroom door was pulled fully open from the outside. A middle-aged Black man in a cook's uniform stared down at them, his expression a mixture of surprise and suspicion.

"What are you girls doing back here?" he asked in a low voice, eyes darting toward the confrontation at the counter. "This isn't a good time to be causing trouble."

"We're not," Maya stammered. "We just... we got lost."

The cook's eyes narrowed. "Lost? In the storeroom of a segregated diner?" His gaze traveled over their modern clothing—Destiny's platform sneakers, Kendra's paint-splattered overalls, Maya's crisp button-down—so out of place in 1960. "And dressed like that?"

"Sir," Kendra began, "we know what's happening out there is important. We don't want to interfere."

He studied them for a long moment. "You talk strange. Where are you from?"

"Orlando," Destiny replied. "Florida."

"Hmm." He didn't seem convinced. "Well, you can't stay here. They've already called the police about those boys at the counter. Last thing we need is more trouble."

As if on cue, the wail of police sirens became audible in the distance.

"Please," Maya said, "we just want to watch. This is... this is history happening."

Something in her words seemed to reach him. The cook's expression softened slightly. "History, huh? You think so?"

"I know so," Maya said with conviction.

He sighed, then motioned for them to follow him. "Come on. There's a better view from the kitchen. But stay out of sight, understand? I don't need to lose my job over three strange girls who don't know how to dress proper."

They followed him through a narrow passage that connected the storeroom to the kitchen. Through a serving window, they had a clear view of the lunch counter and the four young men who sat there with quiet dignity as white customers hurled insults.

"My nephew goes to A&T with them," the cook said quietly, nodding toward the protestors. "Says they've been planning this for weeks. Reading up on Gandhi and such."

"Did you know they were going to do this today?" Kendra asked.

"Word gets around," he replied with a shrug. "Didn't think they'd actually go through with it though." He paused, wiping his hands on a dishcloth. "Name's Henry, by the way. Henry Davis."

"I'm Kendra. This is Maya and Destiny."

Henry nodded, then turned to study them again. "Now, you going to tell me the truth about who you are and how you got in my storeroom?"

The girls exchanged glances.

"You wouldn't believe us if we told you," Destiny said finally.

Henry laughed softly. "Young lady, I'm watching four colored boys sit at a whites-only counter like they have every right to be there—which they do. Today seems like a day for believing impossible things."

Maya hesitated, then reached into her backpack. "We had this book..." she began, but her fingers found only empty space where "The Unwritten History" had been. "It's gone," she whispered.

"What's gone?" Henry asked.

Before Maya could answer, a commotion at the front of the diner drew their attention. Two police officers had entered, nightsticks in hand, scanning the restaurant until their eyes landed on the four students.

"Sir," one officer said, approaching the counter, "we've had reports of a disturbance."

"We're not disturbing anyone," Joseph McNeil replied calmly. "We're just waiting to be served."

The officer's hand tightened on his nightstick. "You know the rules. This counter is for whites only."

"Is there a sign saying that?" Ezell Blair Jr. asked. "I don't see one."

The police officer leaned in closer. "Don't get smart with me, boy."

Maya felt her heart racing. She knew from her history books that the Greensboro Four wouldn't be arrested on this first day—that wasn't how the story went. But seeing the tension firsthand, the naked hatred on the officer's face, made historical certainty feel suddenly fragile.

"I can't watch this," Destiny whispered, turning away from the scene. As she did, her elbow knocked against a stack of metal serving trays, sending them clattering to the floor with a crash that seemed to reverberate through the entire diner.

Every head turned toward the kitchen.

"Stay here," Henry ordered, moving quickly to block them from view. "Don't make a sound."

He stepped through the swinging door into the main diner, plastering on a subservient smile that made Maya's stomach twist with anger and sadness.

"Sorry about that, folks," they heard him call. "Just a little accident in the kitchen."

The second police officer frowned. "Who else is back there, Henry?"

"Nobody, sir," Henry replied smoothly. "Just clumsy old me."

The officer didn't look convinced. "Mind if I take a look?"

"Kitchen's awful messy right now, sir. Health inspector wouldn't like it," Henry said, but the officer was already moving toward the swinging door.

Maya's mind raced. If they were discovered, not only would they be in danger, but they might alter the course of history. The sit-in had to proceed exactly as it had in the history books.

"We need to get out of here," she hissed to her friends. "Now."

Kendra pointed to a back door. "That has to lead outside."

They moved quickly, keeping low, as the swinging door began to open. Just as they reached the exit, Maya glanced back for one last look at the four brave students still seated at the counter. In that moment, one of them—David Richmond—happened to turn his head toward the kitchen.

Their eyes met across sixty years of history, and something like recognition flashed across his face.

Then they were outside, emerging into an alley behind the diner, the February air of 1960 North Carolina crisp against their skin.

"That was too close," Kendra said, leaning against the brick wall of the building.

"Did you see how they just sat there?" Destiny's voice was quiet with respect. "Even with everyone yelling, with the police right there... they just sat there."

"That's courage," Maya replied. "Real courage."

They stood in silence for a moment, processing what they'd witnessed. The alley was narrow, lined with trash cans and delivery crates, the brick walls on either side weathered and aged. A stray cat prowled nearby, eyeing them warily before slinking away into the shadows.

"I wish we could have stayed longer," Maya said finally. "I wanted to see how it ends."

"We know how it ends," Kendra reminded her. "It's in all the history books. They come back day after day. More students join them. The sit-ins spread across the South. Eventually, the stores are forced to desegregate."

"Yeah, but knowing it and seeing it are different," Maya argued. "Don't you want to see their faces when they win?"

"If we didn't get arrested for being weird time-traveling girls first," Destiny pointed out. "Speaking of which, what now? How do we get back to Dr. Freeman's bookstore?"

Maya opened her backpack again, searching futilely for the book that had brought them here. "It's really gone. I don't understand. How are we supposed to get home?"

"Maybe we're not," Kendra said quietly. "Maybe this is what Dr. Freeman meant when she said we needed to learn what history was trying to teach us. Maybe we're stuck here until we figure it out."

The thought hung heavy in the air between them. Stuck in 1960, without money, identification, or any way to explain their presence.

"No," Maya said firmly. "The book brought us here for a reason. There must be a way back."

"Maybe we need to find the book in this time?" Destiny suggested. "Like, maybe it exists here too?"

"Or maybe—" Kendra began, but stopped suddenly, her eyes widening as she stared at something over Maya's shoulder.

Maya turned to see what had caught Kendra's attention. At the end of the alley, a familiar figure stood watching them—Dr. Eleanor Freeman, looking exactly as she had in 2025, her silver-ringed hands clasped before her.

"Dr. Freeman!" Maya called, relief flooding through her.

But as they hurried toward her, the world around them began to shift and blur. The alley stretched impossibly, the brick walls seeming to melt and reform. Dr. Freeman remained in place, her expression serene, as everything else dissolved into swirling colors and fragments of sound.

"Wait!" Destiny cried. "How do we get home?"

Dr. Freeman's voice reached them as if from a great distance. "The journey isn't over. History has more to show you."

The ground beneath their feet vanished, and they were falling again—spinning through time and space, untethered and adrift.

"What's happening?" Kendra shouted, her voice barely audible through the whirlwind.

"I think we're moving again!" Maya called back. "To somewhere else in history!"

They tumbled through the vortex, colors blending and shifting around them, snippets of speeches and music washing over them in waves. A woman's voice singing "Strange Fruit." A deep baritone declaring "I have a dream." The rumble of a crowd chanting "No justice, no peace."

As suddenly as it had begun, the falling sensation stopped. The three girls found themselves sprawled on cold marble flooring in a cavernous, quiet space. The air smelled of polish and paper, and sunlight streamed through tall windows, illuminating dust motes that danced in the still air.

"Where are we now?" Destiny groaned, sitting up slowly and adjusting her jacket.

Maya blinked, taking in their surroundings. They were in what appeared to be a library or museum—rows of glass display cases lined the walls, and informational placards dotted the room.

"I think," she said, her voice echoing slightly in the large space, "we're back in our time. Or closer to it, at least."

Kendra was already on her feet, moving toward the nearest display. "Guys," she called, her voice tight with excitement. "You need to see this."

Maya and Destiny joined her, staring at the glass case. Inside was a familiar book—"The Unwritten History"—its leather cover unmistakable. And beside it, a black and white photograph of four young men seated at a lunch counter.

"The Greensboro Four," Maya whispered. "We were just there."

"Look at the plaque," Kendra pointed.

Maya leaned closer to read the small brass plate: "The Woolworth's sit-in, February 1, 1960, marked a turning point in the Civil Rights Movement. The courage of these four students inspired thousands across the South to join similar protests, ultimately leading to the desegregation of lunch counters and other public facilities."

"We witnessed that," Destiny said softly. "We were actually there."

"And now we're here," Kendra observed, gesturing around them. "But where exactly is 'here'?"

Maya turned slowly, taking in more of the room. On the far wall hung a large banner: "The National Museum of African American History and Culture presents: Pivotal Moments in the Struggle for Equality."

"We're in D.C.," she realized. "The Smithsonian."

"But when?" Destiny asked. "Are we back in 2025?"

Before Maya could answer, the sound of footsteps drew their attention. A tall figure was approaching from the shadows at the far end of the gallery—a well-dressed man with a commanding presence and a voice that Maya recognized instantly when he spoke.

"I see you've found your way to the next chapter," he said, his tone measured and powerful. "But the question is, are you ready to understand what it means to rise up? To speak truth to power, even when that truth might get you killed?"

As he stepped into the light, they could finally see his face—handsome, intense, his eyes burning with purpose and conviction.

"Oh my God," Destiny whispered, visibly stunned. "That's Malcolm X."

Chapter 4
By Any Means Necessary

For several seconds, none of the girls could speak. Malcolm X stood before them—not as a historical photograph or a movie portrayal, but as flesh and blood. His posture was impeccable, his suit perfectly tailored, his gaze intense and evaluating.

"Are you going to stare all day," he asked, "or do you have something to say for yourselves?"

Destiny, never one to be starstruck for long, found her voice first. "We're sorry, Mr. X," she said, then immediately cringed. "I mean, Minister Malcolm. I mean—" She looked desperately at Maya.

"Brother Malcolm," Maya supplied, remembering her father's lectures on proper Nation of Islam honorifics.

Malcolm's eyebrow arched slightly. "You know who I am."

"Everyone knows who you are," Kendra said softly.

His lips curved into what might have been a smile. "Not yet, they don't. But they will."

Maya glanced around the museum gallery, noticing for the first time that something was off. The displays looked newer, the lighting different. And through the windows, she could see cars that belonged to an earlier era.

"This isn't the real museum, is it?" she asked. "This is... somewhere else. Somewhen else."

"Smart girl," Malcolm said. "This building won't exist for decades. But here we are." He gestured around him. "History as you know it. History as I'm living it."

"I don't understand," Destiny said. "If the museum isn't built yet, how are we here?"

"Time isn't linear," Malcolm replied, as if explaining something obvious. "Neither is legacy. Neither is struggle."

"Is this..." Maya hesitated, trying to make sense of it all. "Are you real? Or are you like... a guide? Some kind of construct from the book?"

Malcolm laughed, the sound unexpectedly warm. "As real as you are, which is debatable for all of us at this moment." He checked his watch—a sleek, simple timepiece. "We don't have long. There are things you need to see."

He turned and began walking toward a doorway at the far end of the gallery. After exchanging uncertain glances, the girls followed. As they walked, displays and exhibits flew past at impossible speeds, as if they were fast-forwarding through the museum's contents.

"So you know about the book?" Kendra asked, hurrying to keep up with Malcolm's long strides.

"I know many books," he replied cryptically. "Knowledge, after all, is power."

Destiny leaned close to Maya, whispering, "Okay, but historical significance aside, Malcolm X is fine as hell."

Maya elbowed her sharply. "Show some respect," she hissed, though privately she couldn't disagree.

Malcolm stopped suddenly at a display case containing what appeared to be a simple cup. "Do you know what this is?"

The girls peered at it. There was nothing special about the cup—a ordinary ceramic mug, slightly chipped around the rim.

"A... cup?" Destiny ventured.

"This is the cup I drank from the morning I was murdered," Malcolm said, his voice matter-of-fact. "February 21, 1965. The Audubon Ballroom."

Maya felt a chill run through her. "You know," she whispered. "You know what happens to you."

"Of course I know," he said, eyes never leaving the cup. "I've always known how my story ends."

"Then why don't you stop it?" Destiny blurted out. "If you know, you could prevent it!"

Malcolm turned to her, his expression softening slightly. "Child, death isn't the end of a legacy. Sometimes, it's the beginning." He straightened his already perfect tie. "Now come. We're not here to discuss my future."

He led them through another doorway, and suddenly they were no longer in the museum but standing in the corner of what appeared to be a diner—not unlike the one in Greensboro, but different. The patrons here were all Black, the atmosphere relaxed and communal.

"Chicago, 1955," Malcolm said. "Pay attention."

Through the window, they could see a busy street. People moved along the sidewalks, going about their day. Among them, a boy in a too-large shirt and slacks walked with a jaunty confidence, whistling a tune.

"Emmett," Maya breathed, recognizing him instantly.

"He leaves for Mississippi tomorrow," Malcolm said. "His uncle Mose Wright is waiting for him there. And so is death."

Destiny made a small, pained sound. "Can't we warn him?"

"Would he listen?" Malcolm asked. "Would you have listened at fourteen if strangers tried to tell you your future?"

"We have to try," Kendra insisted.

Malcolm studied them for a long moment. "Very well. But remember—time has its own plans. Its own course."

Before they could ask what he meant, the scene shifted again. They were outside now, on the Chicago street, directly in Emmett's path.

The boy nearly collided with them, stopping short with a laugh. "Whoa! Where'd you all come from?"

Up close, he was even younger-looking than he'd appeared through the window—just a child, really, with bright eyes and an infectious smile. He wore a metal ring with a key on a string around his neck—a detail Maya remembered from history books. His mother had given it to him so he wouldn't lose the key to their apartment.

"Sorry," Maya said, her heart pounding. "We didn't see you."

Emmett grinned. "That's alright. I wasn't watching where I was going either." He tilted his head, studying their clothing with curious eyes. "Y'all ain't from around here, are you?"

"Not exactly," Kendra said.

"We're from Florida," Destiny added, then, unable to contain herself: "You going somewhere, Emmett?"

His surprise at hearing his name quickly gave way to another smile. "How'd you know my name?"

"Lucky guess," Maya said weakly.

Emmett shrugged, accepting this with the easy nonchalance of youth. "I'm headed to the store for my mama. Then tomorrow I'm catching a train down to Mississippi to visit my uncle Mose for two weeks. Never been to Mississippi before."

The girls exchanged glances, the weight of knowledge heavy between them.

"Don't go," Destiny blurted out.

Emmett blinked. "What?"

"To Mississippi," Kendra clarified, her voice gentle but urgent. "Don't go to Mississippi, Emmett. Stay in Chicago."

His brow furrowed in confusion. "Why wouldn't I go? My cousins are down there. It's going to be fun."

"It's... it's dangerous," Maya said, searching for words that might convince him without revealing too much. "The South is different from Chicago. One wrong word to the wrong person..."

"Mississippi is especially dangerous for young Black boys who don't know the unwritten rules," Kendra added.

Emmett laughed, though there was a hint of uncertainty in his eyes now. "My mama already gave me the lecture. Don't look at white folks, say 'yes sir, no sir,' all that. I ain't stupid."

"We know you're not," Maya said, her throat tight. "But please, Emmett. This is life or death. Stay in Chicago."

The lightness faded from his face as he registered their seriousness. "You all are starting to scare me a little. How do you even know who I am?"

"We just do," Destiny said, tears welling in her eyes. "And we know what's going to happen if you go to Mississippi."

"What's going to happen?" he asked, now visibly unsettled.

Maya opened her mouth, but Malcolm was suddenly beside them. "You can't tell him," he said quietly. "That's not how this works."

"Then what's the point?" Destiny demanded. "Why bring us here if we can't save him?"

Malcolm didn't answer, simply watching as Emmett backed away from them, confusion and alarm written across his young face.

"Y'all are crazy," he muttered. "I gotta go."

"Emmett, wait!" Maya called after him. "Just remember—be careful in Mississippi. Don't talk to white women. Don't even look at them. Please."

But he was already hurrying away, occasionally glancing back over his shoulder at the strange girls with their strange warnings.

"Did we change anything?" Kendra asked quietly as they watched him disappear around a corner.

"No," Malcolm said. "You didn't."

"Then why?" Maya demanded, anger flaring. "Why show us this if we can't do anything about it?"

"Because," Malcolm replied, his voice steady, "understanding history isn't about changing it. It's about learning from it."

"That's not good enough," Destiny said, wiping away tears. "He's just a kid."

"Yes," Malcolm agreed, his own expression grave. "A kid who will change the world, though he'll never know it."

The street around them began to shimmer and fade, reality shifting once again.

"You can't save Emmett Till," Malcolm continued as the scene dissolved. "But you can understand what his death meant—what it launched. His mother's courage in showing the world what they did to her son broke open the conscience of a nation."

They found themselves back in the museum, standing before a display case. Inside was a weathered metal casket, a plaque beside it reading: "The original casket of Emmett Till, displayed open at his funeral at his mother's insistence so the world could 'see what they did to my boy.'"

Destiny turned away, unable to look. "This is too much."

"It's history," Malcolm said, not unkindly. "Our history. Painful and powerful."

"Is that why we're here?" Maya asked. "Just to witness horrible things happening to our people?"

Malcolm's expression softened slightly. "No. You're here to understand that every moment of pain in our history is also a moment of profound change. Every martyr creates a thousand activists. Every injustice plants the seeds of future justice."

Kendra, who had been quiet, suddenly looked up. "That's what Dr. Freeman meant. We have to learn what history is trying to teach us."

"Smart girl," Malcolm said again, with a hint of approval.

"But what exactly are we supposed to learn?" Destiny asked, composing herself. "That bad things happen? That people are racist? We already knew that."

"Perhaps," Malcolm suggested, "you're learning that you stand on the shoulders of those who came before. That your 'day off' is possible because of their sacrifices."

The girls fell silent, considering his words.

"Also," Malcolm added, straightening his tie once more, "you're learning that I was indeed, as your friend so eloquently whispered earlier, 'fine as hell.'"

Destiny's mouth fell open. "You heard that?!"

Malcolm's laugh was unexpected and genuine. "Time is fluid here, remember? Nothing escapes my notice."

Maya couldn't help but laugh too, despite the heaviness in her heart. "He's got you there, Destiny."

"I'm not even embarrassed," Destiny declared after a moment of shock. "It's just facts."

Even Kendra cracked a smile, though her eyes remained sad as she glanced back at Emmett's casket.

"So what now?" Maya asked. "More traumatic history lessons?"

"Now," Malcolm said, checking his watch again, "we move forward. You've seen sacrifice. You've seen martyrdom. It's time to see triumph."

The museum around them began to blur once more, colors and shapes melting into one another.

"One more thing," Malcolm called as he too began to fade from view. "Remember that progress isn't a straight line. It spirals, circles back on itself, sometimes retreats before advancing. But it does advance, if you're willing to push it forward. By any means necessary."

As darkness enveloped them, Maya reached out to grasp her friends' hands. Whatever came next, they would face it together.

The last thing they heard before plunging into the void was Malcolm's voice: "Oh, and girls? Don't bother trying to warn Martin about Memphis. I already tried."

Then they were falling again, spinning through time toward whatever lesson awaited them next.

Chapter 5
The Long Walk

This time, the landing hurt.

Maya crashed onto hard-packed dirt, the impact knocking the wind from her lungs. Beside her, Destiny crumpled into an undignified heap of limbs and vintage denim. Kendra somehow managed to land in a crouch, though her grimace suggested it had cost her.

"I am getting really tired of falling through time," Destiny groaned, picking herself up and dusting off her prized jacket. "Can't we just take a bus or something? Time Uber? Anything with cushions?"

Maya sat up slowly, taking stock of her surroundings. They had landed on what appeared to be a rural road, stretching endlessly in both directions. The landscape was sparse and dry, dotted with scrubby trees and low brush. The sun hung oppressively overhead, baking the earth and everything on it.

"Where are we now?" she asked, shielding her eyes against the glare.

Kendra, already on her feet, turned in a slow circle. "I don't know. But it's hot. Really hot."

"And empty," Destiny added, squinting down the deserted road. "No cars, no houses, no nothing."

Maya's mouth felt dry just from the few minutes they'd been here. She checked her backpack—still no book, but she did have a half-full water bottle from their original day off in Orlando. She took a small sip, conscious that they might need to ration it.

"So I guess we just... walk?" she suggested, gesturing toward the road.

"In which direction?" Destiny asked. "It looks the same both ways."

Before anyone could answer, the distant sound of voices drifted to them on the hot breeze. Turning, they saw a small group of people appearing around a bend in the road behind them, moving slowly in their direction.

"Thank God," Destiny sighed. "Maybe they can tell us where we are."

As the group drew closer, details became clearer. There were perhaps a dozen people, mostly Black men and women, with a few white faces among them. They carried signs, though from this distance the words weren't legible, and many wore expressions of determination despite clear exhaustion. Their clothes were stained with sweat, and several limped noticeably.

"I think I know when we are," Kendra said quietly, realization dawning. "It's 1965. The Selma to Montgomery march."

Maya felt a rush of excitement mixed with awe. "Are you sure?"

Kendra nodded, pointing to the approaching group. "Look at the clothes, the signs. And that man in front—I think that's John Lewis."

Sure enough, a young man led the group, his face partially obscured by a bandage wrapped around his head. Despite his injury, he moved with purpose, setting the pace for those behind him.

"Oh my God," Destiny whispered. "Wasn't he almost killed during this?"

"Bloody Sunday," Maya confirmed. "The state troopers attacked the marchers at the Edmund Pettus Bridge. But this must be after that. This is the successful march."

The marchers had noticed them now, curious glances exchanged as they approached the three strangely dressed girls standing in the middle of nowhere.

"What do we do?" Destiny hissed. "What do we say?"

"We join them," Maya said simply. It felt right—if they were meant to witness triumph, walking alongside these civil rights pioneers was surely the way to do it.

The young man at the front of the group slowed as they drew near. Up close, the bandage around his head showed spots of dried blood, and his face bore the marks of recent violence—a split lip, a bruised cheek. Despite this, his eyes were kind as he addressed them.

"Hello there," he said. "Are you joining the march?"

Maya swallowed hard, starstruck in the presence of a man whose face would one day grace history books and congressional halls. "Yes," she managed. "If that's alright."

"Everyone who believes in justice is welcome," he replied. "Though I have to say, you three seem to have appeared out of nowhere."

"We're from Orlando," Kendra explained, the line becoming their standard response across time. "We wanted to be part of this."

If he found anything strange about three teenage girls from Florida suddenly appearing on a remote Alabama highway, he didn't show it. Instead, he simply nodded. "I'm John," he said, offering his hand.

"We know," Destiny blurted, then caught herself. "I mean, we've heard of you. From the news."

John Lewis smiled, though the expression seemed to pain him. "Well, welcome. We're about fourteen miles outside Montgomery now. Should reach the city by tomorrow."

"Fourteen miles?" Destiny repeated, looking down at her platform sneakers with dismay. "In this heat?"

An older woman behind John overheard, her weathered face breaking into a weary smile. "Child, we've already walked forty. Fourteen more is just a stroll in the park."

Properly chastened, Destiny nodded. "Yes, ma'am."

The marchers continued past them, and the girls fell into step with the group. Someone handed them each a small paper cup of water, which they accepted gratefully. Maya noticed that despite the heat and exhaustion, there was an energy to the march—a sense of purpose that transcended physical discomfort.

"You girls picked quite a moment to join," said a white man walking near them, his clerical collar marking him as a minister. "After everything at the bridge, after the long fight for the right to march at all... we're finally going to make it to Montgomery."

"Was it scary?" Kendra asked quietly. "At the bridge?"

A shadow passed over the minister's face. "Terrifying. But sometimes terror is the price of change." He studied them curiously. "You're very young to be out here alone."

"We believe in the cause," Maya said, which wasn't a lie. "Voting rights matter to everyone."

"Indeed they do," he agreed. "Though I must say, your clothes are rather... unusual for marchers."

Self-consciously, Maya glanced down at her white button-down and jeans, Kendra's paint-splattered overalls, and Destiny's vintage jacket—all a far cry from the conservative 1960s attire surrounding them.

"We left in a hurry," she improvised. "No time to change."

The minister seemed to accept this explanation, though his eyes lingered on Destiny's platform sneakers with particular bewilderment.

As they walked, the girls fell into a rhythm, adjusting to the slow, steady pace of the march. The afternoon sun beat down mercilessly, and soon their clothes were damp with sweat, their feet beginning to ache. Maya found herself developing a deeper appreciation for what these marchers had endured—days upon days of this, with the constant threat of violence hanging over them.

"How are your feet holding up?" she asked Destiny after an hour or so.

"They've filed for divorce," Destiny groaned. "They're taking the house, the car, and half my dignity."

A young Black woman walking nearby laughed at this. "First day's the hardest," she said. "I'm Norma. You girls want some of my moleskin for those blisters I know you're getting?"

"Bless you," Destiny said with feeling, accepting the small package Norma fished from her pocket. "I didn't realize how hard this would be."

"Freedom's like that," Norma replied with a shrug. "Harder than you expect, but worth every step."

As they patched their feet and continued walking, Kendra was quiet, her eyes taking in everything—the determined set of the marchers' shoulders, the American flags and hand-painted signs they carried, the way some hummed spirituals under their breath to keep their spirits up.

"I wish I had my sketchbook," she said softly to Maya. "This is... I need to remember every detail."

"We will," Maya assured her. "All of it."

Destiny, who had been suspiciously quiet for the past fifteen minutes, suddenly let out a frustrated groan. "I cannot believe this! We're literally walking with John Lewis during one of the most important civil rights marches in history, and my phone won't work!"

Maya and Kendra turned to see Destiny frantically tapping at her smartphone, holding it up toward the sky as if searching for a signal.

"What are you doing?" Maya hissed, glancing around to make sure no one was paying too much attention.

"Trying to document this for posterity," Destiny replied, as if it were obvious. "Do you know how many followers I could get with authentic footage from 1965? I'd be TikTok famous!"

"Destiny," Kendra said patiently, "even if your phone worked, which it won't because cell towers won't exist for decades, who exactly would you send it to? We're in 1965."

Destiny lowered her phone, her expression falling. "I didn't think of that." Then, perking up: "But when we get back to our time, I could post it then!"

"If we get back," Maya muttered.

The young woman walking nearby—Norma—was watching their exchange with curious eyes. "What's that thing?" she asked, pointing to Destiny's phone.

"It's a... calculator," Maya improvised quickly. "A really advanced one. For math."

"Uh-huh," Norma said, clearly unconvinced. "And it takes pictures too?"

"No!" all three girls said in unison, a bit too forcefully.

Norma raised an eyebrow but didn't press further, simply saying, "Y'all are the strangest volunteers I've ever met."

The day wore on, the miles slowly falling behind them. Occasionally, cars would pass on the highway, some honking in support, others slowing to shout insults or racial slurs. The marchers paid the latter little attention, their focus fixed forward.

As dusk approached, the group began to prepare for another night on the road. Supporters had set up a small camp area ahead, with tents and cooking fires already started. The smell of beans and cornbread wafted through the air, making Maya's stomach growl—she hadn't realized how hungry she was.

"You girls have a place to sleep?" asked an older woman who had introduced herself as Mrs. Jackson. "There's room in my tent if you need it."

"That would be wonderful," Kendra said gratefully. "Thank you."

As they helped prepare the evening meal, the girls found themselves drawn into the community that had formed around the march. People shared stories of where they'd come from and why they'd joined. A group of college students taught them freedom songs. An elderly man who had been born before women even had the right to vote recounted a lifetime of fighting for basic dignity.

"It's like a history book come to life," Maya whispered to her friends as they sat around the fire, bowls of beans balanced on their knees. "But so much more real than anything we could read."

"And painful," Kendra added, nodding toward John Lewis, who sat across the camp, his bandaged head bent in quiet conversation with another marcher. "Those wounds are fresh. This isn't history to them. It's now."

Destiny, who had been uncharacteristically quiet since they'd joined the march, finally spoke. "You know what's messing with me? We know they win. We know they make it to Montgomery, and eventually the Voting Rights Act passes. But they don't know that yet. They're out here risking everything with no guarantee."

Maya considered this. "Maybe that's part of what we're supposed to learn. That change happens because people move forward even without guarantees."

As night fell fully, the camp quieted. Mrs. Jackson showed them to her tent, where bedrolls had been laid out on the ground. It was far from comfortable, but none of the girls complained—not after seeing what the marchers had endured.

"I wonder how long we'll stay here," Kendra whispered in the darkness. "Will we see them reach Montgomery? Or will the book pull us somewhere else first?"

"I hope we stay," Maya replied. "I want to see them win."

"I just hope wherever we go next has indoor plumbing," Destiny muttered, making them all laugh softly.

Sleep came surprisingly easily, the day's exertion overcoming the strangeness of their situation. Maya drifted off to the sound of crickets and distant singing, her dreams filled with marching feet and endless roads.

She woke to shouting.

Bolting upright, it took her a moment to orient herself. The tent was empty except for her and her friends, who were also stirring in confusion. Outside, voices were raised in alarm.

"Get up!" she urged, shaking Kendra fully awake. "Something's happening."

They scrambled outside to find the camp in chaos. People were rushing about, gathering belongings, some pointing down the road where the headlights of multiple vehicles were visible, approaching fast.

"What's going on?" Maya asked a young man hurrying past.

"State troopers," he replied grimly. "And they don't look like they're here to help."

Maya's heart sank. This wasn't right. The third march to Montgomery had been successful. There hadn't been another attack after Bloody Sunday. Had their presence somehow changed history?

"We need to find John," Kendra said urgently. "Or anyone in charge."

Destiny, still groggy from sleep, patted her pockets frantically. "Where's my phone? I need to record this!"

"Will you give it a rest?" Maya snapped, her nerves frayed by the chaos around them. "Your phone doesn't work here, and we might be in actual danger!"

They pushed through the crowd, searching for a familiar face. Finally, they spotted John Lewis helping an elderly marcher to her feet.

"What's happening?" Maya called to him. "Are they going to attack again?"

He looked at her, his expression grim but determined. "We don't know their intentions. But we won't respond with violence, whatever comes."

"But this isn't supposed to happen," Destiny said, forgetting herself. "The march succeeds. You make it to Montgomery."

John gave her a curious look. "Your faith is admirable, young sister. But we can never predict what obstacles might arise on the path to justice."

The approaching vehicles slowed as they neared the camp, their headlights illuminating tense faces. Maya held her breath, expecting the worst. But instead of state troopers, several Black men and women emerged from the cars, carrying boxes and containers.

"It's alright!" someone called out. "It's the support team from Montgomery!"

Relief washed through the camp like a wave. These weren't attackers but allies, bringing fresh supplies and news from ahead.

"False alarm," Kendra sighed, her shoulders slumping with relief.

"Told you," Destiny said, though she too looked visibly relieved. "We're supposed to make it to Montgomery."

Maya wasn't so sure. They had been dropped into this moment for a reason, and she doubted it was just to walk alongside the marchers to a predetermined victory. There had to be something more they were meant to learn or experience.

As the camp settled back into pre-dawn activity, with many too stirred up by the false alarm to return to sleep, Maya found herself drawn to a small campfire where an elderly woman sat alone, her gnarled hands wrapped around a steaming cup.

"Mind if I join you?" Maya asked.

The woman looked up, her dark eyes evaluating Maya before she nodded toward the space beside her. "Been walking long?" she asked, her voice rich with age and a slight accent Maya couldn't place.

"Not as long as most," Maya admitted, sitting cross-legged on the ground. "We just joined yesterday."

"Hmm." The woman sipped her drink. "Young legs. That's good. We need young legs to carry this movement forward."

Something about her demeanor made Maya curious. "How long have you been fighting for civil rights?"

The woman laughed, a dry sound like leaves rustling. "Child, I was born fighting. Came into this world in 1884, on a plantation where my mama and daddy still worked for the family that had owned them. Fighting is all I've ever known."

Maya's eyes widened. "You were born just twenty years after slavery ended?"

"Legally ended," the woman corrected. "But chains take many forms. My grandmama used to tell me about the day they told her she was free. She said it felt like finally being able to take a deep breath after suffocating your whole life."

She paused, studying Maya's face. "You look at me like I'm history come to life."

"You are," Maya said honestly. "I mean—you've seen so much change."

"Some change," the woman agreed. "Not enough. That's why these old legs are still walking." She tilted her head curiously. "What's your name, child?"

"Maya Johnson."

"Well, Maya Johnson, I'm Gertrude Miller. And I've got a feeling about you."

"What kind of feeling?" Maya asked.

Gertrude's eyes seemed to see right through her. "The kind that says you're carrying more than just yourself on this march. Like you've got the weight of understanding on your shoulders." She reached out, her warm hand covering Maya's. "It's a heavy thing, understanding. Especially when you can see both backward and forward at once."

Maya felt a chill that had nothing to do with the pre-dawn air. "I don't know what you mean."

"Yes, you do," Gertrude said softly. "You and your friends aren't from here. I don't mean Alabama. I mean this time."

Before Maya could respond, could even process what the woman had said, Kendra appeared at her side.

"Maya, you need to see this," she said urgently. "They're about to start walking again, and something's happening with Destiny."

Reluctantly, Maya rose, giving Gertrude an apologetic look.

"Go on," the old woman said, waving her away. "But remember what I said. Understanding comes with responsibility."

Maya followed Kendra through the stirring camp to where Destiny stood arguing with a young white reporter who had apparently arrived with the support vehicles.

"—absolute inspiration," the reporter was saying, scribbling in his notebook. "Three young colored girls joining the march. Would make a wonderful human interest piece."

"First of all, we're Black, not colored," Destiny was saying, her hands on her hips. "And second, this isn't about human interest. It's about human rights."

The reporter blinked, clearly thrown by both her terminology and her assertiveness. "I... well, yes, but the readers—"

"The readers need to understand that this march isn't a spectacle," Destiny continued, warming to her theme. "It's not entertainment. It's people fighting for the basic right to participate in democracy. Are you writing this down? Because this is your story right here."

Maya and Kendra exchanged surprised glances. Destiny, whose biggest concern yesterday had been getting a signal on her phone, was now lecturing a 1965 reporter on journalistic ethics.

"She's really going off," Kendra whispered.

"I think she's finding her voice," Maya replied, a smile tugging at her lips.

The reporter seemed equal parts baffled and impressed. "You speak very... differently from the other marchers," he noted.

"Maybe that's because I'm speaking from 2025," Destiny said, then immediately clapped her hand over her mouth, eyes wide.

Maya rushed forward. "What my friend means," she said quickly, "is that she's speaking for the future. For generations yet to come who will look back on this moment."

The reporter squinted at them suspiciously but scribbled in his notebook anyway. "Speaking for the future," he muttered. "Good quote."

As he moved away to interview other marchers, Maya pulled Destiny aside. "What were you thinking? You can't tell people we're from 2025!"

"It just slipped out!" Destiny defended herself. "I got caught up in the moment. He was so... 1965 about everything."

Kendra snorted. "Well, yeah. Because it is 1965."

"You know what I mean," Destiny said. "Anyway, he didn't believe me. Nobody would."

"Gertrude Miller might," Maya said quietly, then explained her strange conversation with the elderly woman.

"You think she knows?" Kendra asked, concern creasing her brow.

"I think she suspects something," Maya replied. "But she doesn't seem bothered by it. Almost like she was expecting us."

Their conversation was interrupted as the call went out for marchers to prepare to move. The camp quickly transformed, bedrolls and tents packed away, breakfast hastily consumed, everyone readying themselves for another day on the road.

John Lewis, his bandaged head making him easy to spot, moved through the group offering encouragement and checking on those who seemed to be struggling. When he reached the girls, he paused.

"How are you three holding up?" he asked.

"Better than expected," Kendra answered honestly. "Though I don't know how everyone does this day after day."

"Faith and purpose make good fuel," he said with a slight smile. "And knowing that what we're doing matters—not just for us, but for those who will come after."

Those who will come after. Like us, Maya thought. Standing here sixty years later because of what these people did.

"Mr. Lewis," she said impulsively, "does it ever scare you? Not knowing if what you're doing will actually change anything?"

He considered her question with the seriousness it deserved. "Every day," he admitted. "But as Dr. King says, faith is taking the first step even when you can't see the whole staircase." He looked at each of them in turn. "Whatever brings three young women to this march—whatever you're searching for—I hope you find it."

With that, he moved on, continuing his rounds through the assembling marchers.

"I think I'm developing a serious historical crush," Destiny whispered, watching him go.

"Better than your Malcolm X crush," Kendra teased. "At least John Lewis is right here where you can make a fool of yourself in person."

"I'm dignified now," Destiny protested. "Didn't you hear me educating that reporter? I'm practically a civil rights leader myself."

Maya rolled her eyes, but she couldn't help smiling. There was something different about Destiny this morning—a shift in her understanding that went beyond jokes.

As the march resumed its slow progress toward Montgomery, the girls found themselves near the middle of the column. The false alarm had energized the group somehow, reminding everyone of the stakes of their journey. People sang as they walked, freedom songs passing up and down the line like currents of electricity.

Maya found herself walking beside Gertrude Miller again, the elderly woman keeping a steady if slow pace, refusing offers of assistance.

"Your friend has a fire in her," Gertrude observed, nodding toward Destiny who was enthusiastically, if somewhat inaccurately, joining in the singing ahead of them. "Reminds me of myself at that age."

"She's always been passionate," Maya agreed. "But seeing all this—being here—I think it's changing her. Changing all of us."

"That's the point of bearing witness," Gertrude said. "You can't remain unchanged once you've truly seen."

They walked in companionable silence for a while, the road stretching endlessly before them. The sun climbed higher, bringing with it the now-familiar heat that made every step an act of will.

"You know," Gertrude said eventually, "my grandmother used to say that time isn't a straight line. Said it was more like a tapestry, with threads weaving back and forth, connecting moments that seem far apart."

Maya's breath caught. "What do you think she meant by that?"

Gertrude gave her a knowing look. "I think you understand her meaning better than most, Maya Johnson."

Before Maya could respond, a commotion rose from the front of the march. People were pointing ahead, voices raised in excitement rather than alarm.

"What is it?" Maya asked, straining to see.

"I believe," Gertrude said with quiet satisfaction, "that's the Montgomery city limits."

Word passed back through the column: they had reached the outskirts of Montgomery. The final stretch of their long journey lay before them. The singing grew louder, the steps more determined despite the exhaustion that marked every face.

Destiny came bounding back to them, her fatigue momentarily forgotten. "We made it!" she exclaimed. "We're actually going to walk into Montgomery with them!"

"Did you doubt it?" Kendra asked.

"No," Destiny admitted. "But knowing something from history books and actually experiencing it are totally different things."

Maya smiled, realizing that this—this insight right here—was perhaps the most important lesson their journey through time could teach them. History wasn't just facts and dates to be memorized; it was real people making hard choices, feeling fear and hope, putting one foot in front of another when the road seemed endless.

As they approached the city proper, the march began to swell with local supporters joining their ranks. What had been hundreds became thousands, a river of humanity flowing toward the Alabama State Capitol.

"This is it," Maya said, a lump forming in her throat as the domed building came into view in the distance. "This is the moment everything changes."

Gertrude Miller, who had witnessed nearly a century of America's painful evolution, reached out and took Maya's hand in her weathered one.

"No, child," she said gently. "This is just one moment among many. The change comes after—in all the small choices people make once the marching stops. In voting booths and classrooms and dinner tables. That's where the real work happens."

Maya looked at the elderly woman with new understanding. "Are you... are you part of why we're here? Like Dr. Freeman and Malcolm?"

Gertrude smiled enigmatically. "I'm just an old woman who's seen too much to be surprised by three girls who speak and dress like they're from another time." She squeezed Maya's hand. "But if I were you, I'd keep an eye out. History has a way of revealing its purpose when you least expect it."

With those cryptic words, she released Maya's hand and continued forward, her back straight despite her years, her eyes fixed on the capitol dome where the next chapter of her people's long struggle awaited.

As they approached the city center, that familiar tingling sensation began at the base of Maya's spine.

"Oh no," she murmured. "Not again."

"What?" Kendra asked, alarmed by Maya's expression.

"I think we're about to jump again," Maya said, keeping her voice low so the other marchers wouldn't hear. "That same feeling is starting."

Destiny groaned. "But we're about to reach the capitol! We've walked like a million miles to get here!"

"I don't think we get to choose," Kendra said, resigned. "The book has its own agenda."

The tingling intensified, spreading through Maya's limbs. The world around her began to waver slightly, colors becoming too bright, sounds simultaneously muffled and sharp.

"Quick, hold hands," she instructed, reaching for her friends. "We need to stay together."

They linked fingers as the march continued around them, the other participants oblivious to the fact that three of their number were beginning to shimmer like heat mirages on summer asphalt.

"Thank you for letting us walk with you," Maya called to Gertrude, who had fallen a few steps behind. "We won't forget this."

The old woman turned, fixing them with one last knowing gaze. "History remembers those who show up," she called back. "No matter when they come from."

And then the ground beneath their feet seemed to dissolve, the sounds of the march fading as if someone were slowly turning down the volume. The last thing Maya saw as reality shifted was the Alabama State Capitol in the distance, its white dome gleaming in the sunlight, and thousands of marchers approaching it in triumph.

Then they were falling once more, spinning through the space between moments, still clutching each other's hands as time itself flowed around them like water.

As he spoke, the commotion around them seemed to slow, then freeze entirely—marchers caught mid-motion, flames suspended in the air, even John Lewis paused in the act of turning away. Only the four of them remained animated in a suddenly still world.

"What did you do?" Maya asked, her voice barely above a whisper.

"I did nothing," Evers said. "Time is simply making room for what needs to happen next."

Dr. Freeman stepped forward, taking Maya's hand in her cool, ring-laden fingers. "You've seen sacrifice. You've seen courage. Now you need to see consequence."

"What does that mean?" Destiny demanded, but even as she spoke, the frozen scene around them began to blur and fade.

"It means," Evers said gravely, "that actions echo across decades. And some fights never truly end."

The world dissolved around them once more, but this time instead of falling, they felt as if they were walking—taking deliberate steps forward even as their surroundings changed.

When the world solidified again, they were standing on a city street. The architecture was modern, the cars familiar. People walked past in contemporary clothing, many looking down at smartphones as they moved.

"We're back in our time," Kendra said, relief evident in her voice.

"Not quite," Dr. Freeman corrected. "Look."

She pointed to a newspaper box on the corner. The front page was clearly visible, the date sending a chill through Maya despite the pleasant temperature: November 8, 2016.

"Election day," she whispered.

"Indeed," Medgar Evers said. "The day many Americans believed the arc of history had bent so far toward justice that it could never bend back."

"Why are we here?" Destiny asked. "This was years before our time."

Dr. Freeman's expression was solemn. "Because to understand triumph, you must also understand how fragile it can be. How progress is never permanent unless you defend it."

As she spoke, a young Black woman walked past them, wearing an "I Voted" sticker proudly on her chest. She was smiling, confident, entirely unaware of what the night would bring.

"She doesn't know," Kendra said softly.

"None of them do," Evers agreed. "Just as those marchers didn't know their victory would one day be threatened by new restrictions, new battles over the very rights they bled for."

Maya felt a weight settling in her chest. "So what's the point then? If even when we win, it can all be taken away again?"

Dr. Freeman's eyes were kind but unyielding. "The point, Maya Johnson, is that the work is never done. Each generation must fight its own battles, must recognize that freedom is not a destination but a constant journey."

"That's exhausting," Destiny said bluntly.

At this, Medgar Evers laughed—a warm, unexpected sound that made several passersby glance in their direction, though none seemed to actually see them.

"Yes," he agreed. "It is exhausting. And necessary. And ultimately, worth every moment of the struggle."

As they stood there, watching people move through a moment that would become its own kind of historical turning point, Maya felt something stirring inside her backpack. Opening it, she found "The Unwritten History" had reappeared, its leather cover warm to the touch.

"It's back," she said, showing her friends.

"That means our journey is nearing its end," Dr. Freeman said. "One more step remains."

"What step?" Kendra asked.

Medgar Evers smiled, and for a moment, Maya could see why he had been such a powerful leader—his presence was at once comforting and galvanizing.

"The step where you decide what to do with everything you've seen," he said. "Where you choose your own place in the unwritten history that lies ahead."

A strange tingling sensation began to spread through Maya's fingertips as she held the book. "I think it's happening again," she warned her friends. "We're about to move."

Destiny quickly turned to Dr. Freeman. "Will we see you again? Will you be there when we get back to the bookstore?"

"Time will tell," was all she said.

"And Mr. Evers?" Kendra asked. "Will we—"

But Medgar Evers was already fading from view, his smile the last thing to disappear as he offered a single parting thought: "Remember, the most dangerous phrase in any language is 'we've always done it this way.'"

Then they were moving once more, but this time it felt less like falling and more like being gently carried forward. The book in Maya's hands glowed with an inner light, illuminating their way through the space between moments.

"Where do you think we're going now?" Destiny asked, her voice sounding distant despite her standing right beside Maya.

"I hope it's someplace with cushioned seating," Kendra replied. "My feet have permanent blisters from all that marching."

Maya wasn't sure what to expect next. This journey through time was clearly far from over, and she suspected they had many more historical moments to witness before they'd understand the book's purpose. As if confirming her thought, the spinning sensation intensified, golden light enveloping them completely.

"Here we go again," she sighed, as they tumbled through the space between moments.

Chapter 6
Hair Raising History

"I'm starting to think we need parachutes for these landings," Destiny grumbled, picking herself up from the polished wooden floor where they had all tumbled in a heap.

This time, their arrival had deposited them behind an ornate folding screen in what appeared to be a well-appointed parlor. Victorian furniture filled the room, alongside potted palms and framed portraits. Through lace-curtained windows, they could see a busy street where horse-drawn carriages and early automobiles shared the road.

"Where are we now?" Kendra whispered, peeking around the screen to make sure they were alone.

"Early 1900s, I think," Maya guessed, taking in the decor. "But where exactly?"

The answer came in the form of voices from the next room—women's voices, engaged in animated conversation. One rose above the others, authoritative and precise.

"The secret is in the formula, ladies. You cannot rush perfection, and you cannot substitute ingredients. That is why Walker's Wonderful Hair Grower stands above all imitators."

The girls exchanged excited glances.

"Madam C.J. Walker," Maya whispered. "We're in Madam C.J. Walker's house!"

"The hair care millionaire?" Destiny perked up immediately. "First self-made female millionaire in America? That Madam C.J. Walker?"

"The very same," Kendra confirmed. "And by the sound of it, we've landed during one of her beauty culture training sessions."

Destiny patted her platform sneakers with new appreciation. "Finally! A historical figure who can appreciate fashion and knows about proper hair care." She fluffed her curls. "I was starting to think we'd only visit historical moments where I'd have to trudge through mud and sleep in tents."

Maya couldn't help but laugh. "So the civil rights movement was just too outdoorsy for you?"

"All I'm saying is that indoor plumbing is also an important historical development," Destiny replied primly. "And I bet Madam Walker has some luxurious bathrooms. Did you know she built a mansion with twenty rooms?"

Before they could decide what to do next, the parlor door swung open. A young Black woman in a neat white uniform entered, then stopped short at the sight of them.

"Oh!" she exclaimed. "I didn't realize anyone was waiting in here." Her eyes traveled over their modern clothing with obvious confusion. "Are you... here for the beauty culture demonstration?"

Maya stepped forward. "Yes," she said, deciding a partial truth was better than none. "We're very interested in Madam Walker's methods."

The woman's brow furrowed. "But the session began an hour ago. And you're not dressed..." She trailed off, clearly struggling to find a polite way to address their bizarre outfits.

"We're from out of town," Kendra offered. "Very far out of town."

"California," Destiny added with authority. "We do things differently there."

"California," the woman repeated doubtfully. "I see. Well, Madam is currently training this month's class of sales agents, but perhaps she could speak with you afterward about enrollment in the next session."

"That would be wonderful," Maya said quickly. "We're happy to wait."

The maid—for that seemed to be her role—nodded hesitantly. "Please make yourselves comfortable. I'll inform Madam of your presence when there's a suitable break."

She left, closing the door behind her, but not before giving them one more bewildered glance.

"California?" Maya whispered once they were alone.

Destiny shrugged. "It was the furthest place I could think of that still exists in this time period. I almost said 'the future,' but I caught myself."

"Growth," Kendra deadpanned, earning her a playful shove from Destiny.

With nothing to do but wait, they explored the parlor, careful not to disturb anything. Kendra gravitated toward the framed photographs, studying the faces of Black women posed proudly in formal attire.

"Look at these," she called softly. "These must be her sales agents and beauty culturists. They look so dignified."

"Because they were making their own money," Maya said, joining her. "Walker didn't just create hair products; she created economic opportunities for thousands of Black women when there were almost none available."

Destiny, meanwhile, had discovered a display of products arranged on a side table—elegant glass bottles and round tins with elaborate labels proclaiming "Walker's Vegetable Shampoo" and "Glossine for the Hair."

"The original Black hair care line," she said reverently, picking up one of the tins to examine it. "My grandma still talks about Walker's products. Says nothing today compares."

The sound of voices grew louder—the meeting in the adjacent room was apparently concluding. The door opened again, but this time it wasn't the maid who entered.

Madam C.J. Walker herself stood in the doorway, an imposing presence despite her small stature. Her dress was impeccably tailored in the fashion of the day, her manner confident and appraising as she surveyed the three strange girls who had appeared in her parlor.

"My assistant tells me you young ladies are from California," she said, her tone making it clear she found this claim dubious at best. "Here to learn about beauty culture."

"Yes, ma'am," Maya managed, finding herself unexpectedly starstruck. "We've heard so much about your methods and your business success."

Walker's expression softened slightly. "Have you indeed? Well, you've certainly come a long way." She moved further into the room, gesturing for them to sit. "Though I must say, your choice of attire is... unconventional."

"It's the California style," Destiny said quickly. "Very avant-garde."

"Hmm." Walker clearly wasn't convinced, but seemed to decide it wasn't worth pursuing. "What interests you about beauty culture? Are you looking to become sales agents yourselves?"

The girls exchanged glances. How much could they say without revealing too much?

"We're interested in how you built your business," Kendra said carefully. "How you created opportunities for Black women."

Walker studied them with increased interest. "Most young ladies come to me wanting to learn how to grow their hair or improve their complexion. Few ask about business strategy right away." She seated herself in a high-backed chair, smoothing her skirts. "You're unusual visitors indeed."

"We believe in economic independence," Maya said, which wasn't a lie. "And we've heard you're the expert."

This earned them a genuine smile. "Well, you've heard correctly. Though I suspect there's more to your story than you're sharing." She leaned forward slightly. "For instance, I'm quite certain that whatever material your shoes are made from hasn't been invented yet."

Destiny instinctively tucked her platform sneakers under the sofa while Maya's mind raced for an explanation.

"The thing is—" she began, but Walker held up a hand to stop her.

"No need to explain," she said surprisingly. "I've had other... unusual visitors. Those who seem out of step with their surroundings. Dr. Freeman warned me you might appear someday."

"Dr. Freeman?" Maya couldn't hide her shock. "Eleanor Freeman? You know her?"

Walker's laugh was rich and knowing. "Eleanor is an old friend—or perhaps I should say a future one. Time is a curious thing in her company."

The girls stared at her in astonishment.

"So you know we're from the future?" Kendra asked hesitantly.

"I suspected as much the moment Lacey described your clothing," Walker confirmed. "Though I admit, I didn't expect you to be quite so young." She gave Destiny a pointed look. "Or quite so fashionable."

Destiny beamed. "I try."

"Well, since we've dispensed with pretense," Walker continued briskly, "why don't you tell me what year you come from, and what brings you to my parlor in particular?"

"We're from 2025," Maya explained. "And we didn't exactly choose to come here. We've been... traveling through different moments in Black history. Learning things."

"2025," Walker repeated thoughtfully. "Nearly a century from now. And are our people faring well in your time?"

The girls exchanged uncomfortable glances.

"Better in some ways," Kendra said diplomatically. "Still struggling in others."

Walker nodded as if this was exactly the answer she'd expected. "Progress rarely moves in a straight line. But tell me," her eyes sparked with curiosity, "do women still use my hair preparations in your time?"

"Well, not exactly the same formulas," Destiny admitted. "But Black hair care is a huge industry. There are thousands of products and brands specifically for our hair. Many founded by Black women entrepreneurs, just like you pioneered."

This seemed to please Walker enormously. "Thousands! Imagine that." She looked at each of their hairstyles with new interest. "And clearly the styles have evolved considerably."

"You have no idea," Destiny laughed. "We have entire social media platforms dedicated just to hair tutorials."

"Social... media?" Walker tested the unfamiliar phrase.

"It's like... a way for people to share information and pictures instantly across the world," Maya tried to explain.

"Ah, like the telegraph, but for frivolities," Walker nodded sagely.

Destiny looked offended. "Hair care is not a frivolity!"

"Of course not," Walker agreed. "It is a path to dignity and economic freedom. Which is precisely why I've dedicated my life to it." She rose from her chair with a decisive movement. "Come, I want to show you something."

She led them from the parlor through a hallway lined with more photographs—Walker with prominent figures of her day, Walker addressing gatherings of immaculately dressed Black women, Walker standing proudly before buildings bearing her name.

"My factory in Indianapolis," she explained, seeing them pause before one image. "Where we manufacture all our preparations. I employ only colored women—over two hundred of them earning good wages."

"That's amazing," Maya said sincerely. "Especially for this time."

Walker gave her a shrewd look. "For any time, I should think. Has the world changed so much that Black women no longer need economic opportunity?"

"No, ma'am," Maya admitted. "That's still very much needed."

They reached what appeared to be Walker's private office—a handsome room with a massive desk, filing cabinets, and walls covered in maps marked with pins.

"Every pin represents a sales agent," Walker explained, gesturing to the maps. "Over twenty thousand women across the country and beyond, each running her own small business, earning her own money, answering to no one but herself."

Kendra moved closer to examine the maps. "You even have agents in Cuba and Panama," she noted.

"Beauty is universal," Walker said simply. "And so is the desire for financial independence."

She crossed to a cabinet and unlocked it with a small key from her pocket. From inside, she withdrew a leather-bound book that looked startlingly familiar.

"The Unwritten History," Maya breathed, recognizing the tome that had started their journey.

"You know it," Walker said, not sounding surprised. "This book has passed through many hands throughout time. It came to me when I was still Sarah Breedlove, washing clothes for a living, my hair falling out from poor diet and harsh lye soap." She ran her fingers over the embossed cover. "It showed me possibilities I had never imagined for myself."

"It's been taking us to different moments in Black history," Kendra explained. "We've seen the Greensboro sit-ins, we met Malcolm X, we even marched from Selma to Montgomery."

"We've also seen some really hard things," Destiny added soberly. "Things I wish hadn't happened to our people."

Walker nodded sympathetically. "History is not always kind, especially not to us. But it is always instructive." She placed the book on her desk. "Would you like to know why you're here, in my parlor specifically?"

"Yes," all three answered in unison.

"Because," Walker said with a smile, "I represent something different from the other moments you've witnessed. I am neither martyr nor marcher. I am a maker."

"A maker," Maya repeated.

"I take what exists and transform it into something better. Hair preparations, yes, but more importantly, women's lives. I take washer-women and maids and farm workers and transform them into businesswomen." Her eyes shone with pride. "In your history books, they may write about my millions, but my true legacy is in the economic foundation I helped build for our people."

"You created generational wealth," Kendra realized. "Not just for yourself but for thousands of families."

"Precisely." Walker seemed pleased by their understanding. "Revolution takes many forms. Sometimes it's a march. Sometimes it's a sit-in. And sometimes," she patted the book, "it's a jar of hair cream that allows a woman to feed her children without depending on anyone's approval."

Maya felt a new appreciation for the various dimensions of resistance and progress they'd been witnessing. "So we're learning about different kinds of change."

"Different tools for different times," Walker agreed. "Though I suspect your journey isn't over yet."

As if responding to her words, the book on the desk began to glow faintly, its cover warming to a gentle shine.

"Ah," Walker said, unsurprised. "It seems you're needed elsewhere."

"But we just got here," Destiny protested. "I have so many questions about your formula! My 4C curls need answers that 2025 still hasn't figured out!"

Walker laughed heartily. "Beauty secrets will have to wait for another time, I'm afraid. The book has its own schedule."

The glow from the book was intensifying, light spilling from between its closed pages.

"Before you go," Walker said quickly, "take this wisdom with you: In your time as in mine, economic power is an essential form of freedom. Remember that as you continue your journey."

"We will," Maya promised, reaching for the book even as the room around them began to shimmer and fade. "Thank you for everything you built."

"One more thing," Destiny blurted as the light grew blinding. "Your hair products—what was actually in them?"

Walker's laugh was the last thing they heard as reality dissolved once more. "That, my dear, remains a trade secret!"

And then they were spinning through time again, Destiny's indignant cry echoing in the void: "A hundred years later and she STILL won't share the formula?!"

The landing this time was soft—almost gentle—as they found themselves sprawled on plush carpet in what appeared to be a modern hotel room. Sunlight streamed through half-drawn curtains, and the distant sound of waves suggested a beachfront location.

"Where are we now?" Kendra asked, sitting up and looking around.

Maya spotted a newspaper on a nearby desk and crossed to examine it. The date stopped her cold: February 25, 2012.

"Guys," she said quietly. "We're in Florida. Sanford, Florida."

Destiny's face fell as understanding dawned. "No," she whispered. "Not this. Not him."

Kendra moved to the window and peered out at the rain-slicked parking lot below. A young Black teenager in a hoodie was crossing toward the hotel entrance, carrying a bag from a nearby convenience store.

"Trayvon," she said softly, her voice catching. "It's Trayvon."

Chapter 7

The Cost of Hoodies

"Oh no," Kendra whispered, the word hanging in the air between them like something fragile and terrible.

Maya felt her heartbeat accelerate as they watched from the hotel room window. A teenager crossed the parking lot below, hood up against the light rain, nothing but a kid heading back from the convenience store with a bag of snacks. An ordinary moment on an ordinary evening that was about to become a tragic milestone in American history.

"We have to warn him," Destiny said, already moving toward the hotel room door.

"Wait," Maya caught her arm. "We don't know what will happen if we interfere."

"I know what will happen if we don't," Destiny shot back, tears forming in her eyes. "We saw what happened with Emmett. We couldn't save him either. I can't just... I can't just watch another Black boy die when we could prevent it."

Maya felt the weight of responsibility crushing down on her. They had already tried to change history once with Emmett, their warnings falling on understandably deaf ears. But could they live with themselves if they didn't at least try to save this young man?

"Let's think about this," Kendra said, always the voice of reason. "The book has been showing us moments we can't change—historical turning points. Maybe we're not supposed to prevent what happens, but to understand it."

"Understand what?" Destiny demanded, her voice rising. "That it's open season on Black boys in hoodies? That hasn't changed from 1955 to 2012 to our time? I understand that just fine without watching it happen!"

Maya moved closer to the window, watching as the teen turned onto the pathway that would take him back to the house where he was staying. In minutes, he would encounter a self-appointed neighborhood watchman who would decide, based on nothing but prejudice and a hoodie, that this boy didn't belong in this gated community.

"I think we're supposed to witness this," she said quietly. "But that doesn't mean we can't try to change it too."

The decision made, they hurried from the hotel room, down the stairs, and out into the rainy February evening. The air was cool but not cold, typical Florida winter weather. They spotted the teen in the distance, walking unhurriedly, probably texting or talking to someone on his phone.

"Hey!" Destiny called, jogging to catch up. "Excuse me!"

He turned, wariness immediately apparent in his posture—the instinctive caution of a young Black man being approached by strangers. When he saw it was just three girls, he relaxed slightly but still kept his distance.

"Yeah?" he asked.

Up close, he was so painfully young—just seventeen, his face still holding traces of childhood beneath the emerging angles of the man he would never get to become. Maya felt her chest constrict with the terrible knowledge of what was about to unfold.

"This is going to sound crazy," Destiny began, "but you need to go straight back to where you're staying. Don't stop, don't talk to anyone, especially not some guy who might be following you."

The teen's expression shifted from cautious to confused. "What? Who's following me?"

"Nobody yet," Kendra said, "but there's a neighborhood watch guy around here who..." She trailed off, unsure how to explain.

"Who what?" he asked, now looking between them with growing suspicion. "Y'all know him or something?"

"No," Maya said, stepping forward. "We just... we know that you might be in danger. There's a man who might think you don't belong here because..." She gestured helplessly at his hoodie.

The teen took a step back. "Is this some kind of joke? Because it's not funny."

"It's not a joke," Destiny said urgently. "Please, just go straight home. Don't confront anyone, even if they confront you first. Call your dad if someone starts following you. Please."

The teen was looking at them like they'd lost their minds, which from his perspective, Maya realized, was a perfectly reasonable conclusion. Three strange girls appearing out of nowhere to deliver cryptic warnings about a man who might or might not follow him because of his hoodie.

"Look, I don't know what kind of game y'all are playing," he said, "but I'm just trying to get back to my dad's fiancée's place. So if you'll excuse me..."

He turned to go, pulling his hood up further against the intensifying rain.

"Wait!" Maya called, desperation making her voice crack. "At least take off the hoodie. Just... just until you get inside."

The teen paused, looking back at them with an expression that mixed annoyance with the faintest hint of concern. "Why? It's raining."

"Because..." Maya struggled for words that wouldn't sound insane. "Because sometimes people make assumptions about young Black men in hoodies. Dangerous assumptions."

Something in her tone must have reached him, because his expression softened slightly. "Yeah, I know all about that. But I can't live my life scared to wear what I want because of what some racist might think."

The simple dignity of his response hit Maya like a physical blow. Here was the cruel paradox—the very conversation they were having highlighted exactly why what was about to happen to him was so unjust, so undeserved, so emblematic of everything wrong with America's perception of Black youth.

"Just be careful," Kendra said softly. "Please."

The teen nodded, clearly still confused but seemingly willing to humor the strange girls. "Always am." He started to walk away, then turned back. "Hey, how do you know my name anyway? Did we meet somewhere?"

Before they could formulate an answer, a car turned slowly into the community entrance behind them, its headlights illuminating the rain. An SUV, moving with the deliberate pace of someone looking for something—or someone.

"Go," Maya urged. "Now. Quickly."

Whether it was her tone or some instinct of his own, the teen seemed to finally sense the urgency. He gave them one last puzzled look, then turned and began walking faster toward his destination.

"Do you think we changed anything?" Destiny asked, watching him disappear around a bend in the path.

"I don't know," Maya admitted. "But we tried."

The SUV crawled past them, the driver—a heavyset man they recognized from news reports that wouldn't exist for weeks yet—barely sparing them a glance. His attention was focused on the path where the teen had gone.

"We should follow them," Destiny said, already starting in that direction.

"And do what?" Kendra asked. "We can't physically stop a grown man with a gun."

"We can call for help," Maya suggested, pulling out her phone. "Call 911."

But the screen remained blank—no service, no connection to the future networks they relied on. Whatever magic allowed the book to transport them through time didn't extend to cellular connectivity.

"Useless," Maya muttered, shoving the phone back in her pocket. "Why bring us here if we can't do anything to help?"

"Maybe that's the point," Kendra said quietly. "Maybe we're supposed to feel this helplessness. To understand that some injustices can't be prevented by individual action alone."

"That's a pretty depressing lesson," Destiny retorted, but her anger seemed to be fading into a resigned sort of grief.

They stood in the rain, uncertain what to do next. Return to the hotel room and wait? Try to follow the teen and the watchman? Neither option seemed right, yet doing nothing felt like a betrayal of everything they'd learned on their journey so far.

"Come on," Maya decided, starting down the path. "We can at least bear witness. We owe him that much."

They followed the winding community paths, the rain soaking through their clothes, the darkness broken only by widely-spaced street lamps. The neighborhood was eerily quiet, most residents tucked safely inside their homes on this wet evening. It felt surreal to be walking these ordinary suburban streets knowing that somewhere nearby, a tragedy was unfolding that would eventually spark protests across the nation.

A sound cut through the patter of rain—raised voices, too distant to make out words but clear enough to convey confrontation. Then a cry, a thud, and the unmistakable crack of a gunshot.

"No!" Destiny gasped, breaking into a run toward the sound.

Maya and Kendra followed, their feet slapping against wet pavement, hearts pounding with dread and useless adrenaline. They rounded a corner to find an open area between two rows of townhomes—and there, in the rain-slicked grass, a scene that would haunt their nightmares.

The teenager lay motionless, the bag from the convenience store scattered nearby—candy and a canned drink spilled across the wet ground like some grotesque still life. Standing over him, gun still in hand, was the neighborhood watchman, his expression a disturbing mixture of shock and self-righteousness.

He looked up as they approached, his hand tightening on the gun. "Stay back!" he shouted. "I've called the police. He attacked me. I was defending myself."

The naked falsehood of his claim, spoken over the body of a boy who had been armed with nothing but candy and a drink, struck Maya with such visceral force that she found herself moving forward despite the gun.

"No, he didn't," she said, her voice steady despite the tears streaming down her face. "He was just walking home. He was just a kid walking home."

"Maya," Kendra warned, trying to pull her back.

But Maya couldn't stop, wouldn't stop. "He was seventeen years old. He was visiting his father. He had every right to be here."

The watchman's face hardened. "You don't know what happened. He was suspicious, walking around looking in windows. When I approached him—"

"When you followed him," Destiny corrected, her voice breaking. "When you hunted him down because you decided his skin and his hoodie made him a threat."

Sirens wailed in the distance—police or ambulance or both, coming too late to save a life but right on time to protect the man who had taken it. Maya knew how this would play out in the coming days and weeks. The shooter wouldn't be arrested that night. The police would accept his claim of self-defense. It would take national outrage and protests to even get charges filed, and even then, a jury would eventually acquit him.

"You're going to get away with this," she said, the knowledge bitter in her mouth. "But we saw. We know what really happened."

The man stared at her, confusion momentarily displacing his defensive posture. "Who are you people? How did you get in here?"

The familiar tingling sensation began at the base of Maya's spine, spreading outward to her fingertips. The world around them wavered slightly, reality beginning to bend and shift as it had so many times before.

"We're leaving," Kendra said urgently, grabbing both her friends' hands. "It's happening again."

But Maya couldn't tear her eyes from the teenager's still form, from the terrible waste of a young life ended by fear and prejudice disguised as vigilance. "We couldn't save him," she whispered. "We couldn't change anything."

"I know," Destiny said, tears mixing with rain on her face. "But we remembered him. We saw him as a person, not just a headline."

The sirens grew louder as the world around them began to dissolve, colors bleeding into one another, solid forms becoming translucent. The last thing Maya saw before reality shifted completely was the watchman's bewildered expression as they literally faded from his sight—one more inexplicable element in a night he would spend the rest of his life trying to justify.

Then they were falling again, tumbling through the space between moments, still clutching each other's hands as if that human connection was the only real thing in an increasingly unreal experience.

The landing, when it came, was jarring—hard-packed earth beneath them instead of wet grass, cool night air replacing Florida's humid warmth. As they struggled to orient themselves, a voice spoke from the darkness.

"You three got any experience with the Underground Railroad? Because we could use some help tonight."

They looked up to see a broad-shouldered Black woman regarding them with curious intensity, behind her a small group of people whose tense postures and wary eyes told a story of desperate flight and precious freedom.

"More time travel?" Destiny whispered, climbing to her feet. "I'm getting really tired of history's magical mystery tour."

"The book must have a reason for bringing us here," Kendra replied, also rising. "Another lesson to learn."

Maya stayed sitting for a moment longer, her mind still replaying the scene they'd just left—the teenager's body, the scattered candy, the rain washing everything clean even as the injustice remained indelible. She wondered if she would ever stop seeing it, if any of them would.

"You okay?" The woman who had spoken extended a hand to help her up, her expression softening slightly at whatever she saw in Maya's face. "I'm Moses, by the way."

"Maya," she replied, accepting her help. "And no, I'm not okay. But I don't think any of us are supposed to be, moving through history like this."

Moses raised an eyebrow. "Moving through history? You talk strange, girl."

"You have no idea," Destiny muttered.

In the distance, dogs barked—a sound that sent visible ripples of fear through the group behind Moses. She turned, suddenly all business again.

"No time for stories now. Patrollers with dogs about two miles back. We need to move." She studied the three girls intently. "You in or out?"

Maya looked at her friends, a silent question passing between them. They were exhausted, emotionally drained from witnessing the senseless death they'd just been powerless to prevent. But perhaps that was precisely why the book had brought them here next—to show them that despite centuries of difference, the struggle continued in new forms. And that individual tragedies, however painful, couldn't be allowed to stop the larger movement toward justice.

"We're in," she said, finding strength she didn't know she still possessed. "Tell us what you need."

As Moses outlined her plan—separating into groups, creating diversions, making for a safehouse with a red barn—Maya felt something shift within her. The weight of witnessing the teen's death didn't lessen, but it transformed somehow, from a paralyzing grief into a fierce determination. They couldn't save everyone. They couldn't change every moment of history. But they could keep moving forward, keep helping where they could, keep bearing witness to both the horrors and the courage.

And perhaps, she thought as they prepared to depart, that was what the book had been teaching them all along—not just about history, but about themselves and their own place in its ongoing story.

Chapter 8
Underground Movements

"I'm starting to think this book has a sick sense of humor," Destiny whispered, her breath forming small clouds in the frigid night air.

The three girls huddled together beneath a canopy of stars so bright and numerous they seemed artificial after the light-polluted skies of their own time. The shock of the young man's death still hung over them like a physical weight, but they had no time to process it—the book had immediately whisked them away, depositing them in what was clearly a very different historical moment.

"Where are we now?" Maya asked, though the heavy darkness, the distant barking of dogs, and the tense expressions on the faces of the small group they'd materialized alongside told a clear story.

"Underground Railroad," Kendra confirmed grimly. "Late 1850s, I'd guess from the clothing. Probably somewhere near the Ohio-Kentucky border."

Their arrival had been typically disorienting—a flash of light, the spinning sensation, and then solid ground beneath their feet. But instead of landing in a museum or bookstore or even a crowded march, they had appeared in the midst of a small group of people moving silently through dense woodland, guided only by starlight and a weathered woman with shoulders as broad as an oak door.

The group had frozen at their sudden appearance, eyes wide with terror, some reaching for concealed weapons. Only the guide's raised hand had prevented outright panic.

"They're friends," she had said with quiet authority, though the suspicion in her eyes made it clear she had no idea who—or what—they were. "The Lord works in mysterious ways, bringing help when we need it most."

That had been nearly an hour ago. Since then, they'd been incorporated into the group without further explanation—seven adults and two children, all escaped slaves making their desperate bid for freedom on the Underground Railroad. The guide, who had introduced herself only as Moses, led them through the forest with the confidence of someone who had walked this path many times before.

Now they had paused in a small clearing, the group catching their breath while Moses conferred with another person who had melted out of the shadows like a ghost.

"I think something's wrong," Maya murmured, watching their serious expressions. "They keep looking back the way we came."

"Patrollers," Kendra suggested. "Slave catchers. They must be following."

Destiny pulled her vintage jacket tighter around herself, shivering not just from the cold. "So what do we do? We can't exactly fight off slave catchers."

"We help however we can," Maya said firmly. "We're here for a reason."

As if on cue, Moses approached them, her face grave in the dim starlight. "You three," she said softly, "you appeared out of nowhere. I don't know what kind of spirits or angels you might be, but we need help."

"We're not—" Destiny began, but Maya cut her off with a quick squeeze of her hand.

"We're here to help," she said simply. "What do you need?"

"Patrollers with dogs about two miles back," Moses explained. "Moving fast. We need to split up to confuse them, but I can't be in two places at once." She studied them intently. "Can you guide some of our friends to the next station? It's a farm with a red barn, about three miles north by northwest."

The girls exchanged glances, a silent conversation passing between them. None of them knew the area, had any wilderness navigation skills, or had ever guided escaped slaves to freedom. But the alternative—declining to help—was unthinkable.

"I can do it," Kendra said, surprising them all. Usually the quietest of the three, she stepped forward with newfound confidence. "I've been sketching maps of everywhere we've traveled. I have a good sense of direction."

Moses nodded, though uncertainty still shadowed her features. "You'll take the Pearson family—mother, father, and the two little ones. They're too slow to keep up with the main group anyway."

"What about us?" Destiny asked, gesturing to herself and Maya.

"You'll create a diversion," Moses said, and something in her tone made Maya's stomach tighten with apprehension.

"What kind of diversion?" she asked.

"The kind that leads those dogs in the wrong direction." She reached into her pack and pulled out two small bundles of fabric. "These are soaked in scent—fox urine mostly. Drag them south for as long as you can, then double back north using the stream to wash away your trail."

"Fox urine?" Destiny recoiled. "You have got to be kidding me."

"This isn't a joke, young woman," Moses said sharply. "There are children's lives at stake."

Destiny straightened, properly chastened. "You're right. I'm sorry." She took one of the bundles, grimacing but determined. "South, then double back using the stream. Got it."

"We'll meet at the red barn," Moses confirmed. "God be with you all."

With that, the group began to split. Moses took three of the adults with her, heading northeast at a brisk pace. Kendra was introduced to the Pearson family—a hollow-cheeked man, his exhausted wife, and two children who couldn't have been more than six and eight. The fear in their eyes made Maya's heart ache.

"You can trust us," she assured them, though she knew how little that promise must mean coming from strange girls in bizarre clothing who had appeared out of thin air.

Mrs. Pearson simply nodded, clutching her children's hands. "The Lord provides," she whispered, though whether she was reassuring Maya or herself was unclear.

"Be safe," Maya told Kendra, hugging her tightly. "We'll see you at the red barn."

"Don't do anything stupid," Kendra replied, returning the embrace. "No heroics."

"Us? Never," Destiny said with a forced lightness that didn't quite mask her fear. She hugged Kendra as well. "Don't get lost."

"I won't." Kendra's voice was steady. "I'll get them there safely. I promise."

Then they were separating, Kendra guiding the Pearson family carefully northwest while Maya and Destiny prepared for their less dignified task.

"I can't believe we're about to run through the woods dragging fox pee," Destiny muttered, holding her bundle at arm's length. "This is so not what I pictured when I said I wanted to connect with my history."

Despite everything, Maya found herself laughing softly. "What, you thought it would all be meeting famous people and witnessing triumphant moments?"

"I mean, kinda?" Destiny admitted. "Not... this."

"History is messy," Maya said, repeating words she'd heard her father say countless times. "And real freedom was never won in comfortable places."

Destiny sighed dramatically. "I know, I know. But did it have to involve animal urine?"

A distant baying of hounds ended their banter. The sound sent ice through Maya's veins—the physical manifestation of human cruelty, trained and weaponized.

"That's close," she whispered. "We need to move. Now."

They set off southward, as instructed, dragging their scent bundles behind them. The forest was pitch black beneath the canopy, roots and undergrowth grabbing at their ankles with every step. Maya had never experienced darkness so complete, so disorienting. Only Destiny's labored breathing beside her confirmed she wasn't entirely alone.

"Stay close," she urged. "We can't afford to get separated."

"Trust me, I'm not going anywhere," Destiny replied, her voice tight with controlled panic. "Especially not alone in a forest in 1850-whatever with slave catchers and their dogs hunting us down."

They pressed on, the terrain growing steadily more difficult—a rocky slope, a tangle of fallen trees, patches of thorny undergrowth that tore at their clothes and skin. The bundle Maya dragged grew heavier with each passing minute, the sharp odor making her eyes water.

"How far do you think we've gone?" Destiny panted after what felt like an eternity.

"Not far enough," Maya replied, pausing to listen. The baying of hounds still carried through the night, but it was difficult to tell if they were getting closer or farther away. "Let's keep going for another ten minutes, then find that stream."

They pushed on, the forest seeming to thicken around them as if conspiring to slow their progress. Just as Maya was about to suggest they change direction, a new sound froze them both in their tracks—voices, human voices, and the jingling of metal.

"Get down," Maya hissed, pulling Destiny behind a fallen log.

They crouched in the underbrush, hardly daring to breathe as lantern light flickered through the trees ahead.

The voices grew clearer—men's voices, rough with excitement and cruelty.

"—can't be far now. Dogs are going crazy."

"Worth a pretty penny, all seven of 'em. Especially them children."

"Master Jenkins gonna pay extra for bringing 'em back unharmed. Fun as it might be to teach 'em a lesson in runnin' away."

The casual malice in the words made Maya's stomach turn. Beside her, Destiny trembled with a mixture of fear and rage.

"Three, maybe four of them," Maya whispered, counting the moving lanterns. "With dogs."

"What do we do?" Destiny's voice was barely audible.

Maya thought quickly. The plan had been to lead the patrollers south, away from both groups of escapees. But they were too close now—if the girls tried to run, they'd be spotted immediately.

"We need a better diversion," she said, an idea forming. "Something that will really draw them away."

"Like what? We don't exactly have flash-bangs or smoke bombs."

Maya's eyes fell on the scent bundles they'd been dragging. "We need to separate. You take both bundles and keep heading south. I'll create a distraction to the east, then double back and meet you at the stream."

Destiny's eyes widened. "No way. We are not splitting up in Nightmare Forest during an active slave hunt. Have you ever seen a horror movie? This is exactly how people die."

"We don't have a choice," Maya insisted. "They're too close. If we both run, they'll catch us for sure."

"And what exactly is your 'distraction' going to be?"

Maya pulled out her phone—useless for calls or internet in 1850, but still equipped with one particularly useful feature. "The flashlight. I'll make them think there's another group heading east. When they follow, you keep going south, then find the stream and head north like Moses said."

Destiny looked torn, clearly hating the plan but unable to suggest a better alternative. "This is insane," she muttered. "But fine. Just... be careful. And if you're not at the stream in twenty minutes, I'm coming back for you."

"Deal." Maya handed over her scent bundle. "Now go, while they're still far enough away."

With one last worried glance, Destiny melted into the darkness, the two bundles dragging behind her. Maya counted to thirty, giving her friend time to put some distance between them, then moved carefully eastward, away from both Destiny's path and the approaching patrollers.

When she judged she was in the right position, she took a deep breath, turned on her phone's flashlight, and swept it briefly through the trees before turning it off again. Almost immediately, the tenor of the voices changed.

"You see that? Light to the east!"

"Split up. Jackson, take two dogs and check it out. Could be another group."

Maya's heart pounded as she heard footsteps and dog paws crunching through underbrush, heading her way. She waited until they were committed to the eastward path, then flashed her light again from a spot twenty yards further on before moving quickly and quietly in a wide arc that would eventually take her back toward the stream.

The ruse worked—too well, in fact. The crash of pursuit followed her, closer than she'd anticipated. A dog barked excitedly, having caught her scent on the natural trail she was leaving.

"This way! Fresh tracks!"

Abandoning stealth for speed, Maya ran, crashing through the underbrush, branches whipping her face, roots threatening to trip her with every step. The forest floor dropped away suddenly, and she half-slid, half-tumbled down a steep embankment, landing painfully at the bottom. A splash told her she'd reached water—not the stream they'd been seeking, but a wider, deeper body. A river.

The voices and dogs were closing in rapidly from above. With no time to find another escape route, Maya made a split-second decision and waded into the cold, dark water. She gasped as it rose quickly to her waist, the current tugging at her legs. The logical part of her brain screamed about hypothermia, drowning risks, and the fact that she'd never been a strong swimmer, but the more immediate threat of capture propelled her forward.

When the water reached her chest, she pushed off from the muddy bottom and began to swim with the current, trying to make as little noise as possible. The frigid water stole her breath, her waterlogged clothes weighing her down as she struggled to keep her head above the surface.

From the bank behind her came shouts of frustration and confusion as the patrollers reached the river's edge.

"Lost the trail!"

"Check up and down the bank! They can't have gotten far!"

"Might've drowned. These runaways don't know how to swim."

Maya let the current carry her around a bend in the river, out of sight of the lanterns. Only then did she angle toward the opposite shore, her arms and legs burning with effort, her lungs screaming for proper breath. When her feet finally touched bottom again, she was shaking so violently she could barely drag herself onto the muddy bank.

She collapsed there, teeth chattering, mind foggy with cold. The realization that she was now completely lost, separated from both Destiny and Kendra, soaking wet in near-freezing temperatures, and being hunted by armed men with dogs filled her with a despair so profound it momentarily paralyzed her.

"Get up," she whispered to herself, her father's voice somehow echoing in her head. "Get up, Maya Johnson. People are counting on you."

Forcing her numb limbs to cooperate, she pushed herself to her feet and tried to orient herself. The river had carried her some distance, but which way was north? Where was the meeting point? Where was Destiny?

A memory surfaced—Kendra enthusiastically explaining navigation by stars during one of their previous jumps. The

North Star, Polaris, always pointed the way. Maya tilted her head back, searching the brilliant star field above until she located the Big Dipper, then traced a line from its outer edge to the North Star.

"That way," she murmured, setting off with faltering steps. She had to find the stream, find Destiny, find the red barn. Had to keep moving or the cold would claim her. Had to warn the others about the patrollers.

She wasn't sure how long she walked, time smearing into a blur of cold and fear and determination. Her wet clothes clung to her body, drawing precious heat away with every step. Branches materialized out of the darkness to scratch her face; roots reached up to trip her feet. Several times she fell, each time rising more slowly than the last.

The sound of running water eventually penetrated her dulled senses. A stream, gurgling softly in the darkness. She had found it—or some stream, at least. But which way to follow it? And where was Destiny?

"Maya!" The whisper came from her left, so unexpected she thought she'd imagined it. "Maya, over here!"

A figure detached itself from the shadows beneath a large tree—Destiny, her face a pale oval in the darkness, her jacket smeared with mud.

"Oh my God," Destiny gasped as Maya stumbled toward her. "What happened? You're soaking wet!"

"Had to swim," Maya managed through chattering teeth. "River. Dogs."

"You're freezing," Destiny realized, immediately shrugging out of her precious vintage jacket. "Here, take this off and put this on."

"N-no," Maya protested weakly. "Your j-jacket."

"Which will be completely useless to me if you die of hypothermia," Destiny said firmly. "Now strip, Johnson. That's an order."

Too cold to argue further, Maya complied, peeling off her sodden button-down and allowing Destiny to help her into the relatively dry jacket. It smelled of fox urine from the bundles, but the residual body heat was heavenly.

"Where d-did you leave the bundles?" Maya asked, her brain slowly beginning to function again.

"About half a mile south of here," Destiny replied, retrieving a large leaf she'd apparently been using as a makeshift cup and filling it with water from the stream. "Drink this. You need to rehydrate."

Maya accepted the leaf-cup with surprise. "When did you get so... survival expert?"

Destiny gave a wan smile. "Turns out my TikTok obsession had an upside. I follow this outdoor survival influencer. Never thought I'd actually need his tips." She refilled the leaf and handed it back. "Drink more. Slowly."

As Maya sipped, Destiny continued, "I dragged those nasty bundles as far as I could, then found the stream like Moses said. I've been waiting here for you for what felt like forever. I was about to go looking when I heard someone coming." Her voice caught slightly. "I was so scared it was the patrollers."

"I'm sorry," Maya said, the enormity of what they were experiencing finally hitting her fully. "This is so much more dangerous than anything we've faced before."

"Yeah, well," Destiny shrugged, trying for nonchalance though her eyes betrayed her fear, "what's a little brush with death among friends? Now, can you walk? We need to find that barn."

"I think so," Maya said, taking an experimental step. Her legs were steadier now, though still weak. "We follow the stream north, right?"

"Northwest, actually," Destiny corrected, pointing. "According to the stars. Remember what my cousin taught me about using the North Star to navigate? The Big Dipper points right to it."

Maya felt a surge of gratitude for her friends—not just for Destiny's unexpected practical skills, but for her surprising knowledge. Maybe they were more prepared for this than she'd thought.

They set off together, following the stream, Maya leaning on Destiny whenever her strength flagged. The night felt endless, the forest a maze of identical trees and shadows. Only the gentle babble of the stream and the steady gleam of the North Star kept them oriented.

"Do you think Kendra made it?" Destiny asked after they had been walking for what seemed like hours. "With the Pearson family?"

"If anyone could get them there safely, it's Kendra," Maya said, believing it completely. "She's always been the one with the best sense of direction."

"And the most common sense," Destiny added. "Unlike us, running around with fox pee and jumping in rivers."

Despite everything, Maya laughed—a small, fragile sound in the vast darkness. "We make quite a team."

"The worst time travelers ever," Destiny agreed with a grin. "But we're still here. Still moving."

The forest began to thin as they continued, the trees growing sparser, the undergrowth less dense. Then, without warning, they emerged at the edge of a large clearing. And there, silhouetted against the star-filled sky, stood a barn. Even in the darkness, they could make out its weathered red boards.

"We made it," Destiny breathed, half in disbelief. "We actually made it."

They approached cautiously, alert for any sign of the patrollers. The barn door was closed, no light visible from within. Maya hesitated at the entrance, unsure of the protocol. Was there a password? A secret knock?

Before she could decide, the door cracked open, and a sliver of lantern light spilled out. A woman's face appeared in the gap, lined with age and suspicion.

"Who's there?" she demanded in a harsh whisper.

"Friends," Maya replied, hoping it was the right response. "Moses sent us."

The door opened wider, revealing a tall, stern-faced white woman in a plain dress and apron. She took in their bedraggled appearance with a mixture of concern and wariness.

"You're with the others?" she asked. "The colored folk Moses was bringing?"

Maya nodded. "Yes. We got separated. Is... is everyone else here?"

The woman's expression softened slightly. "Some. The family with two little ones arrived about an hour ago, with a young woman guiding them."

"Kendra," Destiny breathed in relief. "She made it."

"Come in, quickly," the woman urged, glancing past them at the dark tree line. "Patrollers are thick tonight."

They followed her into the barn, where the warm, musty scent of hay and animals enveloped them. Lanterns had been hung strategically to provide minimal light without being visible from outside. In one corner, the Pearson family huddled together on a pile of blankets, the children mercifully asleep. And sitting beside them, sketching something in the dirt floor with a stick, was Kendra.

She looked up as they entered, her face breaking into an expression of such naked relief that Maya felt her throat tighten with emotion.

"You made it," Kendra said, rising quickly and crossing to embrace them both. "I was so worried."

"You're not getting rid of us that easily," Destiny quipped, though her voice wavered slightly. "Though Maya tried her best by going for a midnight swim in the Ohio River."

Kendra pulled back, noticing Maya's state for the first time. "What happened?"

"Long story," Maya said wearily. "The important thing is we're all here."

"Not all," the white woman corrected grimly. "Moses and the others haven't arrived yet. And dawn's approaching."

Dawn. Maya had lost all track of time in the forest, but now she realized the darkness outside had indeed softened slightly, the stars beginning to fade in the eastern sky. If Moses and the other escapees didn't reach the barn soon, they'd be traveling in daylight—a far more dangerous proposition.

As if summoned by their concern, a soft knock sounded at the barn door. The woman moved quickly to answer it, her hand hovering near what Maya now realized was a small pistol tucked into her apron pocket.

"Friends of a friend," came a low voice from outside—Moses's voice.

The woman opened the door, and Moses slipped inside, followed by... only one other person. The grim set of her mouth told the story before she spoke.

"Patrollers caught two," she said without preamble. "The Jackson brothers. Thomas managed to create a diversion so his brother and I could escape, but they took him."

A strangled cry came from Mrs. Pearson, quickly muffled behind her hand to avoid waking her children. Her husband's face hardened with grief and guilt—survivor's guilt, Maya realized. The guilt of freedom purchased with another's capture.

"We rest here today," Moses continued. "Move on after dark. Next station is two days' travel, but it's across the Ohio River. Free soil."

Ohio. The North. Safety, of a sort.

Maya looked at her friends, a silent question passing between them. Would they still be here tomorrow night? Or would the book whisk them away to another time, another place, before they could see the Pearsons to freedom?

No way to know. But for now, they had made it—all three of them, against considerable odds. They had helped. They had mattered.

The white woman, introducing herself only as "the Friend," brought them stale bread and cold water, then showed them to a pile of hay where they could rest. As exhaustion claimed her, Maya felt Kendra on one side and

Destiny on the other, their presence a comfort beyond words.

"We did it," Destiny whispered in the dim light of early dawn. "We actually helped people escape on the Underground Railroad."

"And almost got caught by patrollers," Kendra added.

"And I swam across what was probably the Ohio River," Maya said, still unable to believe it herself.

"And I used survival skills I learned from TikTok," Destiny concluded with quiet satisfaction. "Just wait until we get back and I can post about this."

"Which you absolutely cannot do," Kendra reminded her.

"I know, I know. But still." Destiny yawned hugely. "We were kind of amazing, weren't we?"

"We were," Maya agreed, feeling sleep tugging at her consciousness. "But mostly we were lucky. And together."

As she drifted off, her last thought was that perhaps this was what they were supposed to be learning through all of these jumps through time—not just about history's grand moments or famous figures, but about themselves. About what they were capable of when they supported each other. About courage and fear and moving forward anyway.

About what it truly meant to be free, and what people would risk to achieve it.

In her dreams, the book waited, its pages turning toward whatever history would show them next.

Chapter 9
Catching Their Breath

Maya woke to the sound of hushed voices. For a moment, she couldn't remember where she was—the straw beneath her, the scent of hay and animals, the dim light filtering through cracks in wooden walls. Then it all came rushing back: the Underground Railroad, the desperate flight through the forest, the ice-cold river.

She sat up slowly, her muscles protesting after the previous night's ordeal. Beside her, Destiny still slept, curled into a tight ball with her arms wrapped protectively around herself. Kendra's makeshift bed was empty.

Maya found her friend sitting with Moses and "the Friend" at a rough wooden table, studying what appeared to be a hand-drawn map. Kendra looked up as Maya approached, her expression a mixture of relief and worry.

"How are you feeling?" she asked.

"Like I decided to swim the English Channel in February," Maya replied, rubbing her arms. "But I'll live."

The Friend—Maya realized they still didn't know her actual name—pushed a tin cup toward her. "Drink. It's just chicory, not real coffee, but it's hot."

Maya accepted the cup gratefully, warming her hands around it before sipping the bitter liquid. It wasn't coffee as she knew it, but the warmth spreading through her chest made it the best thing she'd tasted in a long time.

"We were just discussing the next leg of the journey," Kendra explained, gesturing to the map. "The Pearsons and Isaiah need to reach the next station before continuing to Canada."

"Canada," Maya repeated. The word sounded impossibly distant in this context—not just a friendly neighboring country, but a promised land of freedom.

Moses nodded gravely, her weathered face solemn. "Only true safety for a runaway. Even in the free states, slave catchers can claim their 'property' under the Fugitive Slave Act."

The casual reference to human beings as property made Maya's stomach turn, though she knew it was simply the legal reality of this time. She studied the map, noticing the route marked in faded ink.

"How much further to Canada?" she asked.

"About two hundred miles," the Friend answered. "But with help along the way." She gave the girls an appraising look. "You three are the strangest conductors I've ever seen on the railroad. Where did Moses find you?"

Before any of them could formulate an answer, Destiny's voice came from behind them.

"We found each other," she said, shuffling toward them with her hair spectacularly disheveled, eyes still heavy with sleep. "Fate, I guess. Or something like it."

"Destiny," Maya said with relief. "How are you feeling?"

"Like I slept in a barn after running through a forest dragging fox pee," Destiny replied, wrinkling her nose. "So basically accurate." She eyed the cup in Maya's hand. "Is that coffee? Please tell me there's more."

The Friend poured another cup of the chicory brew and handed it to Destiny, who took a cautious sip and then made a face.

"This is not coffee," she declared. "This is tree bark juice pretending to be coffee."

"Destiny!" Kendra hissed, embarrassed.

But the Friend actually chuckled. "An accurate assessment. Real coffee is hard to come by these days, especially for those of us who refuse to purchase goods produced by slave labor."

This silenced Destiny, who took another sip with a more contemplative expression.

"An abolitionist household," Maya observed.

"For three generations," the Friend confirmed with quiet pride. "My grandmother hid the first runaways in this very barn. My father expanded the hidden cellar beneath us. And now I continue their work."

Maya felt a surge of admiration for this woman and the risks she took. In this era, helping escaped slaves could mean fines, imprisonment, or worse.

"You're very brave," she said.

The Friend shook her head. "Brave is running hundreds of miles to freedom with patrollers at your back. Brave is leaving everything you've ever known for a chance at liberty. I merely provide a way station."

From the corner of the barn, a child's voice rose in a brief whimper, quickly hushed by a mother's soothing tones. The Pearson children were waking, their faces still marked by the exhaustion and fear of their journey.

"Those poor kids," Destiny murmured. "They should be worrying about, I don't know, toys and games or whatever kids did in the 1800s. Not running for their lives."

"Children on plantations rarely have childhoods," Moses said, her deep voice somber. "They're property from birth."

The stark reality of those words hung heavy in the air. Maya tried to imagine what it would be like to grow up knowing you were owned, that your body and labor belonged to someone else. The thought was so alien, so fundamentally wrong, that her mind rebelled against it.

"What happens now?" Kendra asked, redirecting the conversation to practical matters.

"Now we wait," the Friend replied. "The next leg of the journey must happen at night. Today, everyone rests."

"And us?" Maya asked, the question directed at her friends more than their hosts. Would they still be here by nightfall? Or would the book pull them elsewhere before then?

As if summoned by her uncertainty, the familiar tingling sensation began at the base of her spine, spreading outward to her fingertips. She met Kendra's eyes and saw the recognition there.

"It's happening again," Kendra said quietly.

Destiny groaned. "Already? I haven't even finished my fake coffee."

Moses and the Friend looked between them in confusion. "What's happening?" the woman asked.

"We have to go," Maya explained, standing quickly. "I'm sorry—we can't really explain. But thank you, for everything you're doing."

"But the Pearsons—" Moses began.

"Will make it to freedom," Kendra assured her with a certainty born of historical knowledge. "The Underground Railroad will succeed, Moses. More people than you can imagine will find their way to freedom because of conductors like you."

The tingling intensified, the barn around them beginning to waver and blur. Maya reached for her friends' hands, forming their now-familiar circle as reality started to shift.

"Wait," the Friend called, her voice already sounding distant. "Who are you? How do you know these things?"

"We're just students," Maya replied as the world began to dissolve around them. "Learning our history, one moment at a time."

Then they were falling again, tumbling through the space between moments, hands clasped tightly together as they had learned to do. This time, however, the sensation was different—less like being pulled and more like being gently set down. The landing, when it came, was the softest they'd experienced yet.

Maya opened her eyes to find herself sitting in a comfortable armchair. Not lying on the ground, not sprawled awkwardly, but properly seated, as if she'd been placed there with care. Beside her, in identical chairs, Kendra and Destiny blinked in similar confusion.

"Well, that was new," Destiny remarked, looking around. "At least we didn't land in a heap this time."

They appeared to be in some kind of office or study—bookshelves lined the walls, a large desk dominated one corner, and a coffee table sat between their chairs, bearing a silver tray with a teapot and cups. Sunshine streamed through tall windows framed by heavy curtains.

"Where are we?" Kendra wondered, her artist's eye taking in the details of the room—the ornate moldings, the Persian rug, the oil paintings in gilt frames.

Before either of her friends could venture a guess, the door opened, and a familiar figure entered—Dr. Eleanor Freeman, her silver rings catching the light as she crossed to the desk.

"Welcome back," she said, as if they had merely stepped out for a moment rather than traveled through decades of history. "I trust your journey has been educational so far."

The girls stared at her in shocked silence.

"Dr. Freeman?" Maya finally managed. "But... how? When are we?"

"New York City, 1917," Dr. Freeman replied, setting down a folder she'd been carrying. "And as for how, well, that's a rather complicated explanation that we don't have time for at the moment."

"How are you here?" Destiny demanded. "You were in Orlando in 2025, then you showed up in that Montgomery museum in the 60s, and now you're in 1917? Are you time traveling too?"

Dr. Freeman's lips quirked in a hint of a smile. "In a manner of speaking. Though my relationship with time is... different from yours."

"You've been guiding us," Kendra said, realization dawning. "The book—it's been taking us to specific moments, hasn't it? This isn't random."

"Nothing about history is random," Dr. Freeman replied cryptically. "Every moment connects to every other, forming patterns for those who know how to see them." She poured tea into three cups, adding milk and sugar with practiced grace. "But enough about me. You three look like you've had quite an adventure since our last meeting."

Maya accepted the offered cup, struck by the surreal contrast between their night on the Underground Railroad and this civilized tea service. "That's putting it mildly," she said. "We've seen... so much."

"Tell me," Dr. Freeman prompted, settling into a chair across from them.

They took turns recounting their experiences since leaving Dr. Freeman at the Selma to Montgomery march—their meeting with Madam C.J. Walker, the heartbreaking encounter with Trayvon, and most recently, their night guiding escapees on the Underground Railroad.

Dr. Freeman listened without interruption, her expression revealing nothing of her thoughts. When they finished, she nodded slowly.

"You're beginning to understand," she said. "The connections between moments, the through-lines of history."

"What I understand," Destiny said, setting down her teacup with unusual deliberation, "is that we keep witnessing terrible injustices without being able to change anything. We couldn't save Emmett, we couldn't save Trayvon, we couldn't even stay long enough to make sure the Pearsons reached Canada safely."

"And is that what you believe your purpose is?" Dr. Freeman asked. "To change history?"

"Isn't it?" Maya challenged. "What's the point of sending us to these moments if we can't help?"

"Perhaps the help isn't meant for them," Dr. Freeman suggested. "Perhaps it's meant for you—and through you, for others."

The girls fell silent, considering this perspective.

"You mean we're supposed to learn from these experiences," Kendra said slowly. "Carry the knowledge forward."

"Knowledge alone is passive," Dr. Freeman corrected gently. "What matters is how it transforms you—and what you do with that transformation when you return to your own time."

Maya felt something shift in her understanding. They weren't just witnesses to history but carriers of its lessons, tasked with translating past struggles into future action.

"So what now?" she asked. "Another historical tragedy to observe?"

Dr. Freeman's expression softened slightly. "I think you've earned a brief respite. A chance to see another side of our history—not just the struggles, but the triumphs as well." She rose and crossed to a cabinet, withdrawing three garment bags. "Which is why I've arranged for you to attend a gathering tonight at a friend's home in Harlem."

"A gathering?" Destiny perked up visibly. "Like a party?"

"A salon," Dr. Freeman clarified. "A meeting of minds—artists, writers, musicians, thinkers. The beginnings of what will later be called the Harlem Renaissance."

Kendra's eyes widened. "We're going to witness the Harlem Renaissance firsthand?"

"Its early days, yes." Dr. Freeman laid the garment bags across a nearby sofa. "Madam Walker sends her regards, by the way. She was disappointed she couldn't host you herself, but she's traveling on business at the moment. She did, however, ensure you would have appropriate attire for the occasion."

"You know Madam Walker?" Maya asked, then immediately felt foolish. Of course Dr. Freeman knew historical figures across time—that much was becoming clear.

"We correspond regularly," Dr. Freeman replied with a slight smile. "She was quite impressed by your visit to her parlor."

Destiny moved to inspect the garment bags, unzipping one to reveal a shimmering evening dress in deep blue, styled in the fashion of 1917. "Oh my God," she breathed. "Is this for us?"

"You can hardly attend a Harlem salon in jeans and fox-urine-scented jackets," Dr. Freeman said, a hint of amusement in her voice. "There's a bathroom through that door where you can freshen up. The gathering begins at eight."

"Tonight?" Maya asked, suddenly nervous. "But we don't know anything about how to behave in 1917 society. What if we say or do something wrong?"

"You've navigated a Woolworth's lunch counter in 1960, a plantation in Mississippi, and the Underground Railroad," Dr. Freeman reminded her. "I think you can manage a dinner party."

"Will you be coming with us?" Kendra asked.

Dr. Freeman shook her head. "I have other matters to attend to. But don't worry—your host knows to expect you." She moved toward the door, then paused. "One more thing. The book will remain here, in my safekeeping, until tomorrow. Tonight is for experience, not for study."

With that cryptic remark, she left, closing the door softly behind her.

The girls looked at each other, processing this new development.

"So... we're going to a Harlem Renaissance party," Destiny said slowly. "In 1917. In fancy dresses." A grin spread across her face. "This might be the best jump yet."

"It's not a party, it's a salon," Kendra corrected, though she couldn't hide her own excitement. "A gathering of intellectuals and artists. Do you realize who might be there? Langston Hughes, Zora Neale Hurston, Claude McKay..."

"Duke Ellington, Louis Armstrong," Maya added, catching the enthusiasm. "This could be amazing."

"And no one's chasing us with dogs or guns," Destiny pointed out, already unzipping the other garment bags to examine their contents. "Plus, look at these dresses! This is the cultural experience I signed up for."

Maya ran her fingers over the fine fabric of a burgundy dress that looked to be her size. After the hardships they'd witnessed, the prospect of experiencing a joyful, creative moment in Black history felt like a gift.

"I guess we've earned a night off from watching historical tragedies," she said.

"We absolutely have," Destiny agreed emphatically. "One night to experience the good stuff—the art, the music, the culture." She struck a dramatic pose with the blue dress held against her. "Besides, can you imagine the TikTok I could make about attending an actual Harlem Renaissance salon? If only my phone worked in 1917."

Kendra rolled her eyes, but she was smiling. "Always thinking about social media."

"Hey, I'm just saying," Destiny defended herself, "some experiences deserve to be shared. And this is definitely one of them."

As they gathered the dresses and moved toward the bathroom to clean up, Maya felt a lightness she hadn't experienced since their journey began. Tonight wouldn't erase the painful realities they'd witnessed, but perhaps it would remind them that Black history contained joy and creation alongside struggle and resistance.

They had walked with civil rights marchers, sat with protestors, fled with escaped slaves. Now they would dance and converse with the artists and thinkers who had crafted a cultural renaissance. The full spectrum of their people's experience in America—that, Maya realized, was what Dr. Freeman wanted them to understand.

"What do you think she meant about the book staying here?" Kendra asked as they examined the vintage cosmetics laid out on the bathroom counter.

"I think she means we're actually staying put for once," Maya replied. "Twenty-four whole hours in one time period. No sudden jumps, no running for our lives."

"Just music, art, literature, and fancy dresses," Destiny added, twirling with her garment bag. "I can live with that."

For the first time since touching the book in Dr. Freeman's store, Maya felt she could take a full breath, could set aside the weight of witnessing history's darkest moments and simply experience one of its brightest. Tomorrow would bring new challenges, new moments to observe and learn from. But tonight—tonight was for celebration.

"Well," she said, feeling a smile spread across her face, "I guess we better get ready for the Harlem Renaissance."

Chapter 10
Renaissance Rising

"If I could just figure out how to smuggle this bathtub back to 2025, I'd be set for life," Destiny sighed, sinking deeper into the clawfoot tub filled with steaming, lavender-scented water. "Indoor plumbing might be the greatest achievement of human civilization."

From the adjoining room, Maya's laugh drifted through the partially open door. "Better than the smartphone you can't stop complaining about not working?"

"At this exact moment? Yes." Destiny swirled the water around her shoulders. "I've spent the last week—day?—time period?—whatever—swimming through a freezing river, being chased by slave catchers, and trudging through mud in the rain. I deserve this."

She wasn't wrong. Dr. Freeman's New York brownstone had proven to be a sanctuary of unexpected luxury after their harrowing experiences. Each girl had been given her own bedroom with an attached bathroom, complete with modern—well, modern for 1917—amenities. After quick, whispered negotiations, they'd agreed Destiny should bathe first, given her still-obvious distress about the teenager in Florida.

"Don't use all the hot water," Kendra called from where she sat cross-legged on the bedroom floor, sketching furiously in a leather-bound book Dr. Freeman had provided. "Some of us are still wearing eau de Underground Railroad."

"There's plenty," Destiny assured her, reluctantly rising from the tub. "Though I still can't believe we're actually going to a Harlem Renaissance party tonight. Like, the actual Harlem Renaissance. With actual Langston Hughes and Zora Neale Hurston. Potential Harlem Renaissance. Whatever."

"Salon," Kendra corrected automatically, not looking up from her drawing. "Not a party. An intellectual and artistic gathering."

"Potato, po-tah-to," Destiny replied, wrapping herself in a plush towel. "Either way, we're going to need these dresses."

The garments Madam Walker had sent hung from a standing rack in the corner—three evening dresses in richly colored silks and velvets. Maya was already examining the burgundy one, running her fingers over the intricate beadwork along the neckline.

"These must have cost a fortune," she murmured. "Especially in 1917."

"Madam Walker doesn't do anything halfway," Kendra observed, finally looking up from her sketchbook. "Remember her factory? Her mansion? She believes in making statements."

"Speaking of statements," Destiny emerged fully dressed in a robe, toweling her hair, "how exactly are we supposed to act tonight? I don't know the social rules for 1917. What if I say something scandalous without realizing it?"

"Just follow my lead," Maya suggested, laying the burgundy dress carefully across the bed. "My dad's a history professor, remember? I grew up watching more historical documentaries than cartoons."

"Yeah, but watching isn't the same as doing," Destiny pointed out. "What if I use the wrong fork? Or talk to some man I'm not supposed to talk to? Or—"

"Since when are you worried about social etiquette?" Kendra interrupted, her eyebrows raised in genuine surprise. "You're the one who told our vice principal his tie looked like 'something a cat threw up' last semester."

"That was different," Destiny insisted. "That was just school. This is... this is history. These are going to be famous people, important people, and they don't even know it yet." She flopped dramatically onto the bed beside the dress. "I don't want to embarrass us."

Maya and Kendra exchanged glances of mild astonishment. Destiny Turner—confident, outspoken, never-met-a-social-boundary-she-wouldn't-cross Destiny—was nervous about making a good impression.

"You'll be fine," Maya assured her, sitting beside her on the bed. "Besides, this is the beginning of the Harlem Renaissance. People were breaking social rules left and right. That was kind of the point."

"Really?" Destiny perked up.

"Really," Maya confirmed. "This was a time of experimentation, of pushing boundaries. Black artists and intellectuals were redefining what was possible, creating new forms of expression." She grinned. "So in a way, your complete lack of filter might actually be historically appropriate."

"Well, when you put it that way..." Destiny's usual mischievous smile returned. "I guess I can work with that."

Kendra rolled her eyes but couldn't hide her own smile. "Just try not to cause an international incident. My turn for the bath."

As Kendra disappeared into the bathroom, Destiny examined the blue silk dress clearly intended for her. "You know what's weird?" she said, suddenly thoughtful. "I keep thinking about the people we've met. Moses and the Friend and the Pearsons. Malcolm X. That teenager in Florida. I wonder if they ever think about us after we disappear."

"I've been wondering the same thing," Maya admitted. "Do we leave any mark at all? Or does history just... reset once we're gone?"

"Maybe we're meant to be forgotten," Destiny suggested. "Like, maybe that's part of the deal. We get to witness history, but we don't get to change it or be part of it."

"That's depressing."

"Tell me about it." Destiny held the dress against herself, examining her reflection in the full-length mirror. "Though I have to admit, history has better fashion than I expected. This is gorgeous."

The dress was indeed beautiful—midnight blue silk that shifted to a deep teal in certain lights, with delicate silver beading creating a starburst pattern across the bodice. It was designed in the fashion of 1917—ankle-length with a slightly raised waistline, and a scooped neckline that was modest by modern standards but would have been considered daring for the time.

"I wonder if Dr. Freeman told Madam Walker our sizes or if this is just another mystery of time travel," Maya mused, picking up her own burgundy dress again.

"Speaking of mysteries," Destiny said, lowering her voice despite the running bath water that would mask their conversation, "what do you make of Dr. Freeman? The way she pops up throughout history? The way she knows where we'll be and when?"

Maya shook her head. "I don't know. At first, I thought she was just the bookstore owner who happened to have a magical book. But now..." She trailed off, uncertain how to articulate her thoughts.

"Now it seems like she's orchestrating everything," Destiny finished for her. "Like she's not just sending us through time, but guiding us through specific moments for a reason."

"But what reason?" Maya wondered. "What's the point of all this? What are we supposed to be learning?"

"Maybe there's no grand lesson," Destiny suggested with uncharacteristic seriousness. "Maybe it's just about experiencing history firsthand, about understanding in a way you can't from textbooks."

"Maybe," Maya agreed, though she wasn't convinced. There was a pattern to their jumps, a purpose she couldn't quite grasp yet but could feel taking shape with each new experience.

The bathroom door opened, releasing a cloud of steam as Kendra emerged wrapped in a towel. "Your turn, Maya," she said. "And hurry. According to that fancy clock downstairs, we have less than two hours before we need to leave for this salon."

Maya gathered her toiletries—provided by Dr. Freeman, who seemed to have thought of everything—and headed for the bathroom, pausing at the door. "Hey, Destiny?"
"Hmm?"

"You're going to be amazing tonight. Just be yourself."

Destiny's smile was surprisingly vulnerable. "Thanks. I'll try not to start any cultural movements before their time."

"Wouldn't that be something," Maya laughed. "Destiny Turner: The secret influence behind the Harlem Renaissance."

As Maya closed the bathroom door, she heard Kendra say, "Don't encourage her. She already thinks she should have a Wikipedia page."

"I absolutely should!" Destiny's indignant reply was the last thing Maya heard before the rushing water drowned out their voices.

An hour and a half later, three very different young women from 2025 stood transformed into visions of 1917 elegance.

Maya's burgundy dress complemented her rich brown skin perfectly, the beadwork catching the light with every movement. Kendra wore forest green velvet that made her eyes appear almost golden in contrast. And Destiny, true to form, had managed to accessorize her blue silk with a dramatic silver headband she'd discovered in a drawer—a bit flashier than the conservative style of the day, but striking nonetheless.

"We clean up pretty good for time travelers," Destiny declared, twirling experimentally and watching the silk swirl around her ankles.

"The shoes are killing me though," Kendra complained, shifting her weight awkwardly in the T-strap heels that had come with the dresses. "How did women in this era function in these?"

"They didn't run through forests or swim across rivers," Maya pointed out, adjusting a pin in her upswept hair. "They mostly sat and conversed politely."

"Boring," Destiny declared. "No wonder they needed a Renaissance."

A soft knock at the door heralded Dr. Freeman's arrival. She entered looking not at all like a mysterious time-traveling guide but very much like a sophisticated Harlem socialite of 1917. Her silver hair was elegantly styled, and she wore a deep purple dress with an Egyptian-inspired collar of hammered silver that matched her many rings.

"My," she said, surveying them with evident approval, "you three certainly adapted quickly."

"These dresses make it easy," Maya replied, though in truth, the transformation went deeper than clothing. Something about being here, in this time, in this house, had shifted their perspectives. The horrors they had witnessed—the Greensboro sit-in, the killing in Florida, the desperate flight on the Underground Railroad—felt simultaneously ever-present and somehow distant, as if the book had granted them the ability to hold multiple realities in their minds at once.

"Our carriage awaits," Dr. Freeman announced. "Are you ready for your introduction to the Harlem Renaissance?"

"As ready as we'll ever be," Kendra answered for all of them. "Though I still have questions about—"

"All in good time," Dr. Freeman interrupted smoothly. "Tonight is for experience, not explanation."

The carriage turned out to be a gleaming black automobile—one of the first Model Ts, Maya guessed, though modified with custom details that suggested significant wealth. A uniformed driver held the door as they carefully arranged their dresses to avoid wrinkling.

"So whose salon are we attending exactly?" Maya asked as the automobile pulled away from the brownstone.

"A'Lelia Walker's," Dr. Freeman replied. "Madam Walker's daughter. She's becoming quite the patron of the arts, hosting gatherings in her home for Black intellectuals, writers, and musicians."

"The Dark Tower!" Kendra exclaimed, then looked embarrassed at her outburst. "Sorry—that's what her salon will be called later. It becomes famous as a gathering place during the Renaissance."

Dr. Freeman's lips twitched in amusement. "Indeed. Though at this point, in 1917, it's still rather informal. The full flowering of the movement is still a few years away. Consider this... a preview of what's to come."

The girls fell silent as the automobile navigated the streets of Harlem. Through the windows, they caught glimpses of a neighborhood in transition—elegant brownstones alongside tenement buildings, smartly dressed professionals walking past laborers returning from long days of work. Signs of migration were everywhere in the fresh-off-the-train expressions of newcomers from the South, carrying suitcases and hope in equal measure.

"So many people," Destiny murmured, pressing closer to the window. "It's like the whole world is coming to Harlem."

"In a way, it is," Dr. Freeman confirmed. "The Great Migration is bringing thousands of Black Southerners north every month. Harlem is becoming the capital of Black America—culturally, politically, intellectually."

"It's one thing to read about it," Maya said softly, "and another to see it happening."

The automobile turned onto a tree-lined street of impressive townhouses and stopped before one particularly grand specimen. Light blazed from every window, and the sound of piano music drifted into the night air.

"Oh my God," Destiny whispered, suddenly gripping Maya's hand. "We're really doing this."

"Remember," Dr. Freeman said as the driver opened the door, "you are my nieces visiting from Boston. Your father is a professor at Howard University, which explains your education and manners. Beyond that, be yourselves—within reason," she added with a pointed look at Destiny, who managed to look both innocent and offended simultaneously.

"What am I going to do, start twerking in the middle of a 1917 salon?" she whispered to Maya as they followed Dr. Freeman up the steps.

"With you? Always a possibility," Maya whispered back, earning herself an elbow in the ribs that she had to pretend was a stumble on the unfamiliar shoes.

A butler greeted them at the door, taking their light wraps and Dr. Freeman's calling card before ushering them into a foyer of imposing elegance. From there, they could see into a large parlor where perhaps thirty people were gathered in small conversational groups, drinks in hand, the air hazy with cigarette smoke.

"Dr. Freeman!" A tall, striking woman in gold silk approached, arms outstretched in welcome. "I was thrilled to receive your note. And these must be your nieces from Boston?"

"A'Lelia," Dr. Freeman embraced her warmly. "Yes, allow me to introduce Maya, Kendra, and Destiny. Girls, our hostess, Miss A'Lelia Walker."

The girls curtseyed as they'd hastily practiced before leaving the house, earning an approving nod from Dr. Freeman.

"Such lovely young women," A'Lelia commented, her kohl-rimmed eyes taking in every detail of their appearance. "And so fortunate to have an aunt who believes in exposing youth to culture. Please, make yourselves comfortable.

There are refreshments in the dining room, and many interesting people to meet."

With that, she swept away to greet other guests, leaving the girls momentarily at a loss.

"What do we do now?" Kendra asked under her breath.

"Mingle, I suppose," Maya replied, equally uncertain despite her earlier confidence.

Destiny, however, had already spotted the refreshment table. "I vote we start with food. Historical experiences always make me hungry."

Before they could follow her lead, Dr. Freeman intercepted them. "I'll be catching up with old friends," she said, her emphasis on "old" carrying meaning only they would understand. "Feel free to explore, but remember—observe more than you speak, especially around the gentlemen. It's 1917, and certain... freedoms you're accustomed to haven't arrived yet."

With that cryptic warning, she glided away, immediately engaged in conversation by a distinguished-looking man with silver temples.

"What did she mean by that?" Destiny asked, rejoining them with a small plate of finger sandwiches.

"I think she means don't flirt with men from 1917," Maya translated dryly. "Different rules."

"As if I would," Destiny sniffed, though her eyes were already tracking a handsome young man in a perfectly tailored suit who was gesturing animatedly as he spoke to a small group. "Though some historical research might be educational..."

"Destiny," Kendra hissed. "Focus. We're here to observe the beginning of one of the most important cultural movements in Black history, not for you to try out vintage dating techniques."

"Why not both?" Destiny grinned, but her attention was already shifting as a distinguished older man at the piano finished his piece and a young man rose to take his place. "Oh, they're going to play something else!"

The young pianist—barely older than the girls themselves—settled at the keys and after a moment's concentration, launched into a piece that seemed to defy categorization. It contained elements of classical music, certainly, but underneath ran currents of something wilder, more improvisational, with syncopated rhythms that made Maya's feet want to tap in time.

"What is that?" Destiny whispered, entranced. "It's not quite ragtime, but it's not classical either."

"Jazz," Kendra breathed. "Early jazz. It's still evolving in 1917, but that's definitely jazz we're hearing."

Around the room, reactions varied. Older guests looked somewhat scandalized, while younger ones leaned forward in their seats, clearly captivated by the innovative sounds. Maya noticed A'Lelia watching the crowd's response with a slight smile, as if the mixed reaction was exactly what she'd hoped for.

"She's pushing boundaries," Maya realized aloud. "Testing how far she can go."

"Smart," Kendra agreed. "Introducing new art forms in small doses, in private settings, before taking them public."

"I don't care about the strategy," Destiny said, swaying slightly to the rhythm. "I just want to dance to this."

"Not appropriate for young ladies in 1917," Maya reminded her. "At least not in this setting."

"Then this setting needs to evolve faster," Destiny muttered, though she settled for subtle shoulder movements that wouldn't draw undue attention.

As the evening progressed, they circulated cautiously through the salon, eavesdropping on conversations that ranged from passionate debates about art and politics to whispered gossip about who in the room was secretly funding radical publications. They observed A'Lelia working the room with practiced skill, introducing like-minded individuals and then stepping back to watch creative connections form.

In one corner, a heated discussion about poetry was underway.

"The sonnet form is inherently European," a bespectacled young man was arguing. "To truly express the Black experience, we need new forms, new rhythms that reflect our own cultural heritage."

"Nonsense," countered an older gentleman. "Mastery of traditional forms proves our equal intellectual capacity. Innovation can come later."

"Later?" A young woman in a daring sleeveless dress interjected. "While white critics continue to dismiss our work as primitive or exotic? No, we need to redefine the rules now, create art that defies their expectations and forces them to engage with our humanity on our terms."

Maya nudged Kendra. "That's Jessie Fauset," she whispered. "She'll become the literary editor of The Crisis magazine. She published some of the most important writers of the Renaissance."

The debate continued, growing more passionate by the minute, drawing a larger audience that included several white patrons of the arts who seemed torn between discomfort and fascination at the frankness of the discussion.

"They don't realize they're witnessing the birth of a movement," Kendra observed quietly.

"But we do," Maya replied, feeling a strange sense of privilege and responsibility in that knowledge.

Meanwhile, Destiny had somehow managed to strike up a conversation with a young woman arranging refreshments on a side table. From their animated gestures and occasional laughter, it appeared they were getting along famously despite the supposed social barriers.

"Leave it to Destiny to find a friend wherever we go," Kendra said with a mixture of exasperation and admiration.

"It's her superpower," Maya agreed. "Though Dr. Freeman is giving her the eye."

Indeed, across the room, Dr. Freeman had noticed Destiny's socialization with the staff and was subtly shaking her head in warning. Destiny, naturally, pretended not to notice.

"Should we rescue her?" Kendra asked.

"From which one?" Maya laughed. "Dr. Freeman or the new friend?"

Before they could decide, a hush fell over the room as A'Lelia stepped forward, tapping a spoon against her crystal glass for attention.

"Friends, we have a special treat tonight," she announced. "As many of you know, I've been corresponding with a promising young poet from St. Louis who has recently moved to New York. He's graciously agreed to share one of his new works with us this evening. Please welcome Mr. Langston Hughes."

A slender young man rose from a corner seat, clutching a worn notebook. He couldn't have been more than twenty, his face still bearing traces of boyhood despite his formal attire. He looked nervous but determined as he took his place at the center of the room.

Maya felt goosebumps rise on her arms. Langston Hughes—the Langston Hughes—about to recite a poem that might not even be published yet, might not even be in his collected works. They were witnessing literary history in the making.

"This is a work in progress," Hughes began, his voice soft but carrying clearly in the suddenly silent room. "It's called 'The Negro Speaks of Rivers.'"

As he read, his voice grew stronger, more confident, the words flowing like the rivers he described. Maya found herself holding her breath, transported by the power and beauty of the verse.

"I've known rivers ancient as the world and older than the flow of human blood in human veins..."

When he finished, the room remained silent for one breathless moment before erupting in applause. The young poet looked startled, then pleased, a smile breaking across his face that transformed him from nervous youth to the confident artist he would become.

"That poem will be famous," Maya whispered to her friends. "It will be taught in schools for generations."

"And we just heard it first," Kendra replied, her eyes wide with wonder.

Destiny rejoined them, somehow having acquired a glass of what looked suspiciously like champagne. "Did you see that? Did you hear that? That was Langston Hughes!"

"Where did you get that?" Maya hissed, nodding at the glass.

"My new friend Lucille thought I looked thirsty," Destiny replied with an innocent smile. "Don't worry, it's mostly water. I think. Anyway, who cares? We just heard Langston Hughes read a poem that's going to be famous for a hundred years!"

Her enthusiasm was impossible to resist, and Maya found herself grinning despite her concerns about historical propriety. This was why they were here, after all—to experience these moments firsthand, to feel the electricity in the air as a new cultural movement took shape around them.

As the evening continued, more performances followed—a singer whose voice made Kendra tear up, a dramatic reading of a short story that had the room alternately laughing and gasping, and more of that proto-jazz piano that had Destiny nearly bouncing in her seat.

"I wish we could stay here," she sighed as the clock approached midnight. "This is the first jump that hasn't involved mortal danger or watching horrible injustices. I could get used to 1917 Harlem."

"Until you wanted to vote, or work outside approved professions, or wear pants," Kendra reminded her. "Rose-colored glasses, much?"

"You know what I mean," Destiny protested. "This—" she gestured around the vibrant salon, "—this joy, this creativity, this community. This is what I want to remember about our history."

Maya nodded, understanding perfectly. After all they had witnessed—the brutality of slavery, the terror of the Underground Railroad, the long march to voting rights, the senseless death of a boy in a hoodie—this celebration of Black culture and intellect felt like coming up for air after nearly drowning.

"Every struggle we've seen led to this," she said quietly. "Without the people who ran north, who marched, who sat at lunch counters, who fought and died for basic rights, this room wouldn't exist. This freedom to create, to express, to reimagine what's possible—it was bought with all those sacrifices."

Her friends fell silent, absorbing this connection that somehow made both the struggles and the triumphs more meaningful. The pattern of their journey was beginning to make sense—not random jumps through history but a carefully constructed narrative showing both the pain and the purpose, the cost and the reward.

"Dr. Freeman knows exactly what she's doing," Kendra said, as if reading Maya's thoughts. "She's telling us a story through time."

"Our story," Destiny added. "Not just about famous people or big events, but about all of us, across generations."

The weight of that realization settled over them, profound yet somehow comforting. They were part of something larger than themselves, connected to both past and future in ways they were only beginning to understand.

A'Lelia approached, interrupting their contemplation. "You girls seem deep in thought," she observed with a warm smile. "Are you enjoying the evening?"

"It's magical," Maya replied honestly. "Thank you for including us."

"Any relation of Eleanor's is welcome in my home," A'Lelia assured them. "Though I must say, you three have the most interesting way of observing a room. Almost as if you're witnessing history rather than simply attending a gathering."

Something in her tone made Maya wonder if A'Lelia, like her mother, somehow sensed their unusual circumstances. But before she could formulate a response, Dr. Freeman appeared at A'Lelia's side.

"These girls have always been unusually perceptive," she said smoothly. "Their father encourages a certain... historical perspective."

"How fortunate for them," A'Lelia replied, her knowing gaze shifting between the girls. "To have such guidance." She touched Dr. Freeman's arm lightly. "Eleanor, dear, I simply must introduce you to Mr. Garvey. He's just arrived from Jamaica with the most fascinating ideas about pan-African unity."

As the women moved away, Maya caught Dr. Freeman glancing back with an expression that clearly said, "Stay out of trouble."

"Too late for that warning," Destiny murmured. "We're literally time travelers crashing a Harlem Renaissance salon."

"Speaking of time," Kendra said, nodding toward a grandfather clock in the corner, "it's nearly midnight. How long do these things usually last?"

"In this era? Well into the morning," Maya replied. "But I'm guessing we'll be leaving when Dr. Freeman is ready."

As if summoned by her words, the now-familiar tingling sensation began at the base of Maya's spine. "Or not," she amended, grabbing her friends' hands. "I think the book has other ideas."

"Now?" Destiny protested. "But I haven't even tried dancing to that jazz music yet! And Langston Hughes was going to read another poem!"

"I don't think we get to vote," Kendra said, her voice tight as the tingling intensified. "Quick, let's move somewhere less visible."

They slipped through a side door into what appeared to be a library, dark and unoccupied. Just in time, too, as the world around them began to waver and blur at the edges.

"I'm not ready to leave," Destiny admitted, her earlier enthusiasm fading to regret. "I wanted more time here."

"Me too," Maya agreed, feeling the pull of the time shift growing stronger. "But maybe that's the point. To leave us wanting more, to remind us that joy was as much a part of our history as struggle."

"To show us what we're fighting for," Kendra added softly.

As the library dissolved around them, replaced by the now-familiar vortex of time and space, Maya's last thought was of Langston Hughes's face as he finished his poem—young, hopeful, unaware of the impact his words would have across decades. How many other moments of creation and joy had their journey through the harder parts of history made possible?

And where would the book take them next?

Chapter 11
Human Calculators

The landing was gentle this time—almost as if the book had decided they deserved a break after their series of rough arrivals. Maya found herself standing upright rather than sprawled on the ground, and her friends' similar expressions of surprise suggested they'd had equally soft landings.

"Well, that's new," Destiny remarked, straightening her vintage jacket. "Usually I need a chiropractor after these jumps."

"Small mercies," Kendra agreed, looking around. "Where are we now?"

They appeared to be in a long corridor with mint-green walls and speckled linoleum floors. The institutional feel was unmistakable—some kind of government building,

Maya guessed. Large windows along one wall revealed a parking lot filled with cars that looked like they belonged in an old movie—rounded bodies in pastel colors, gleaming chrome bumpers, and massive fins.

"Check out those cars," Destiny said, moving to the window. "We're definitely back in time again. Those are like, I don't know, 1950s Cadillacs or something?"

"Mid-1950s, I think," Kendra confirmed, her artist's eye taking in the details. "Look at our outfits."

Maya glanced down and realized with surprise that their clothing had changed. Instead of the elegant 1917 dresses they'd been wearing at the Harlem salon, they were now dressed in 1950s attire—full skirts, button-up blouses with peter pan collars, and sensible shoes. Maya's outfit was a deep burgundy that complemented her skin tone, Kendra wore forest green, and Destiny, naturally, had somehow ended up in a fashionable turquoise ensemble complete with a matching headband.

"Okay, this is new," Maya said, turning in a circle to examine her outfit. "The book's never changed our clothes before."

"Maybe it's learning," Kendra suggested. "After all the strange looks we've gotten showing up in modern clothes."

"I'm not complaining," Destiny declared, admiring her reflection in the window glass. "This look is actually cute. Very vintage chic." She struck a pose that would have been perfect for Instagram, had her phone been working. "Although these shoes are not it. Who decided women should wear torture devices disguised as footwear?"

Maya rolled her eyes but couldn't suppress a smile. Even time-traveling through America's most pivotal historical moments, Destiny still found ways to critique the fashion.

The corridor was eerily quiet. No one in sight, just the distant hum of what sounded like massive machines and the occasional click-clack of what might be a typewriter from behind closed doors.

"Should we explore?" Destiny asked, already inching down the hallway. "I mean, that's why we're here, right? To figure out what historical moment we've landed in?"

Maya nodded her agreement, noticing a framed portrait on the wall—President Eisenhower looking solemnly down at them. "Eisenhower administration, so between 1953 and 1961."

"Also, look at this," Kendra pointed to a bulletin board where a notice announced: "NACA Employee Picnic, Saturday July 14, 1956."

"NACA?" Destiny repeated, brow furrowed. "What's that?"

"National Advisory Committee for Aeronautics," Maya explained, excitement building as she put the pieces together. "It's what NASA was called before it became NASA in 1958."

"NASA?" Destiny's eyes widened. "Are we at like, space headquarters or something?"

"Langley Research Center in Hampton, Virginia," Maya confirmed, recognizing the building's architecture from documentaries she'd watched with her father. "This is where they did the calculations and testing for the early space program."

"Calculations," Kendra repeated, a look of dawning comprehension on her face. "Maya, is this—"

Before she could finish her question, a door at the far end of the corridor swung open, and a Black woman in a crisp skirt suit emerged, arms laden with folders and notebooks. She walked with purpose, her low heels clicking rhythmically against the linoleum. As she drew closer, her eyes widened slightly at the sight of the three teenagers standing awkwardly in the middle of the hallway.

"Are you the new secretarial trainees?" she asked, her voice carrying a hint of a Southern accent. "You're supposed to report to Mrs. Mitchell in Personnel, not wander the computing section."

"Uh, no ma'am," Maya replied quickly. "We're actually... visitors. We got a bit turned around."

The woman's eyebrows rose. "Visitors? We don't get many visitors here, especially not..." she hesitated, her eyes taking in their clothing, "...young ladies in this section."

"We were invited by..." Destiny began, clearly improvising, but was saved from having to invent a name when another door opened and a voice called down the hallway.

"Dorothy! Did you bring those trajectory calculations? Dr. Stafford is waiting."

The woman—Dorothy—turned and called back, "Coming, Mary! Just give me one moment." She returned her attention to the girls, her expression softening slightly. "Look, you really shouldn't be in this section without badges. Are you here for the school tour program?"

"Yes!" Kendra seized the explanation gratefully. "That's exactly right. We got separated from our group."

Dorothy nodded, her suspicion fading to mild exasperation. "That happens every time. The tour guides move too quickly, and these hallways all look the same." She shifted her armload of folders to check her watch. "The tour groups usually gather in the main lobby before heading to the viewing area for the test launches. If you hurry, you can probably catch up with them."

"Thank you," Maya said sincerely. "We appreciate your help, Miss...?"

"Mrs. Vaughan," the woman corrected gently. "Dorothy Vaughan."

Maya froze, recognition flooding through her. Dorothy Vaughan—one of NASA's pioneering Black female mathematicians, a "human computer" whose calculations were vital to America's space program. They had landed at Langley during the early Space Race.

"It's an honor to meet you, Mrs. Vaughan," she said, unable to hide the reverence in her voice.

Dorothy gave her a curious look, but before she could respond, the door down the hall opened again and another Black woman emerged, this one wearing cat-eye glasses and an impatient expression.

"Dorothy, what's the holdup? The engineers are waiting for those calculations, and you know how they get when—"

She stopped, noticing the teenagers. "Who are these young ladies?"

"Lost students from the tour group, Mary," Dorothy explained. "I was just directing them back to the main lobby."

Mary approached, studying them with sharp, intelligent eyes that seemed to miss nothing. "Well, they've wandered into quite a restricted area. Not many visitors make it to the West Computing section." She looked directly at Maya. "What school are you from?"

"Lincoln High," Maya improvised, naming her own school and hoping it existed in whatever year they'd landed in.

"Lincoln?" Mary's eyebrows rose. "That's over in Hampton, isn't it? You girls have come a long way for a tour." Her tone suggested she wasn't entirely convinced by their story.

"We're very interested in mathematics and space exploration," Kendra offered, which wasn't exactly a lie.

This seemed to catch Mary's interest. "Are you, now? That's refreshing. Most girls your age are more concerned with finding husbands than calculating orbital trajectories."

"Not us," Destiny declared with such conviction that both women smiled. "We're more interested in making history than dinner."

Dorothy laughed outright at this. "Well said, young lady." She glanced at Mary. "Reminds me of someone else I know."

Mary's expression softened fractionally. "Perhaps. Though I hope she's better at following rules than I was at her age." She checked her watch. "We really need to get these calculations to Dr. Stafford, Dorothy. The girls can find their way back."

"Actually," Maya said impulsively, "could we ask you a few questions first? For our school report?" She ignored Kendra's warning glance. "We're specifically researching women in mathematics and science."

The two women exchanged looks—surprise mixed with something that might have been pleasure at being the subject of such research.

"I suppose I could spare five minutes," Mary conceded. "Dorothy, go ahead without me. Tell Stafford I'll be right there with the final figures."

As Dorothy continued down the hall, Mary gestured for the girls to follow her into a small office. Inside, the walls were lined with bookshelves crammed with technical manuals and mathematical textbooks. A desk dominated the center of the room, covered with graph paper, slide rules, and stacks of calculation sheets filled with neat, precise handwriting.

"I'm Mary Jackson, by the way," she said, perching on the edge of her desk. "I work in the computing pool here at NACA."

Maya and Kendra exchanged excited glances, while Destiny looked between them in confusion.

"Is that name supposed to mean something to me?" Destiny whispered, too quietly for Mary to hear.

"Hidden Figures," Kendra whispered back. "She's one of the Black female mathematicians who calculated the trajectories for the space program."

Destiny's eyes widened in recognition. "Oh! The movie with Taraji P. Henson and Janelle Monáe!"

"What exactly do you do here, Mrs. Jackson?" Maya asked, ignoring their sidebar conversation.

"I'm a computer," Mary replied. "We all are, in the West Computing section."

"You mean... you use computers?" Destiny asked, genuinely confused.

Mary laughed. "No, dear. We are the computers. Human computers. We perform the mathematical calculations for the engineers—everything from wind tunnel data analysis to trajectory computations." She gestured to the stacks of paper. "All by hand. Every equation, every variable, calculated manually."

Destiny stared in what could only be described as horror. "By hand? As in, with actual pencils and paper? No calculators?"

"Well, we have slide rules," Mary replied, holding up a complex-looking ruler with multiple sliding sections. "And calculating machines for some tasks. But yes, most of our work is done manually."

"But that's..." Destiny seemed at a loss for words, which Maya could hardly believe was possible. "That's like... impossible. I can't even calculate a tip without my phone."

Mary's brow furrowed. "Your phone?"

"She means she's not good at mental math," Maya interjected quickly. "We rely on... tools... a lot in our generation."

"I see," Mary said, though she clearly didn't. "Well, mental calculation is a skill like any other. It improves with practice."

"How accurate do your calculations need to be?" Kendra asked, examining a sheet of equations with genuine interest.

"Extremely," Mary replied, her expression serious. "When you're calculating the trajectory for a test aircraft—or eventually, a spacecraft—the slightest error could be catastrophic. Lives depend on our precision."

"And you do this all day?" Destiny couldn't seem to get past this point. "Calculate things? Without, like, technology to help you?"

"It's not just calculating, it's problem-solving," Mary corrected. "We develop the mathematical approaches needed to answer questions that have never been answered before. How do you calculate the heat shield requirements for a capsule reentering Earth's atmosphere? What adjustments are needed for a safe orbital trajectory? These aren't simple arithmetic problems."

"I once spent twenty minutes trying to figure out how to split a dinner bill three ways," Destiny admitted. "And I still overcharged Kendra by five dollars."

"Which you never paid back," Kendra muttered.

Mary looked between them with growing amusement. "Mathematics isn't for everyone, I suppose. Though I find that most people who claim they're 'bad at math' simply haven't been taught properly."

"Or they have a calculator app that does it for them," Destiny said under her breath, earning an elbow from Maya.

"So you're a mathematician?" Maya steered the conversation back on track.

"I have a degree in mathematics and physical science from Hampton Institute," Mary confirmed. "Though what I really want is to be an engineer." Her voice took on a determined edge. "I've applied for the training program, but there are... obstacles."

The girls knew what those "obstacles" were—segregated education, discrimination, separate facilities. History would record that Mary Jackson would eventually become NASA's first Black female engineer, but only after petitioning the City of Hampton to allow her to take graduate courses at the all-white Hampton High School.

"You'll do it," Destiny said with absolute conviction. "You'll be an engineer. I know you will."

Mary studied her curiously. "Your confidence is touching, if perhaps overly optimistic. There's never been a female engineer here, let alone a colored one."

"You'll be the first," Maya said, unable to help herself. "You'll make history."

Something in her tone must have conveyed her certainty, because Mary's expression shifted from skepticism to thoughtful consideration.

"Perhaps," she said finally. "It won't be easy."

"Nothing important ever is," Kendra replied.

A knock at the door interrupted their conversation. Dorothy poked her head in, looking slightly frantic.

"Mary, they're asking for you now. Dr. Stafford is having a fit about these launch calculations."

Mary stood immediately. "I need to go. It was... interesting meeting you girls. I hope you enjoy the rest of your tour." She paused at the door. "And good luck with your school report. I'm flattered to be included."

As the door closed behind her, Destiny let out a breath. "Oh my God. We just met Mary Jackson. THE Mary Jackson. Hidden Figures Mary Jackson!"

"And Dorothy Vaughan," Maya added, equally awed. "Two of the most important women in NASA's early space program, and almost nobody knew their names until decades later."

"Until that book and movie came out," Kendra agreed, moving to examine the papers on Mary's desk more closely. "They calculated the trajectories for the Mercury and Apollo missions, right?"

"Among other things," Maya confirmed. "Without their calculations, John Glenn wouldn't have orbited the Earth, Neil Armstrong wouldn't have walked on the moon."

"And they did it all by hand," Destiny said, picking up a slide rule and examining it with baffled respect. "No computers, no calculators, no apps. Just their brains and pencils and paper." She set the slide rule down carefully. "Meanwhile, I once failed a math test because my calculator batteries died."

"You failed because you didn't study," Kendra corrected dryly.

"Details, details," Destiny waved a dismissive hand. "The point is, these women were doing rocket science with basically the equivalent of an abacus!"

"And doing it while dealing with segregated bathrooms, segregated cafeterias, segregated computing sections," Maya added. "Having to be twice as good to get half the recognition."

Destiny picked up one of the calculation sheets, squinting at the complex equations that filled the page. "I can't even understand what I'm looking at. It's like hieroglyphics."

"It's calculus," Kendra explained, peering over her shoulder. "Differential equations, by the look of it."

"You understand this?" Destiny asked incredulously.

"Some of it," Kendra admitted. "I take AP Calculus, remember? But this is way beyond high school level."

"Let me see," Maya joined them, studying the neat columns of numbers and symbols. "I think this is calculating how much heat a spacecraft would generate on reentry into the atmosphere. See these variables here? They're tracking velocity against atmospheric density."

Destiny stared at her friends as if they'd suddenly started speaking Martian. "You two are freaking me out right now. Since when are you NASA-level math geniuses?"

"We're not," Kendra laughed. "Not even close. That's what makes what these women did so incredible. They were solving problems no one had ever solved before, with no computers to check their work."

"And if they made a mistake, astronauts could die," Maya added soberly.

Destiny shuddered. "No pressure or anything."

Curiosity getting the better of her, Maya opened one of the desk drawers, finding more calculation sheets, paperclips, and a small framed photograph of a young girl—Mary's daughter, she guessed. Another drawer contained what appeared to be course materials—advanced engineering textbooks and notes written in Mary's precise handwriting.

"She's already studying engineering on her own," Maya observed. "Preparing for when she gets the chance to take those classes."

"That's determination," Kendra said admiringly. "Not just dreaming about breaking barriers but doing the work in advance so she's ready when the opportunity comes."

"I can't even prepare for tests I know are coming," Destiny admitted. "I'm pretty sure I've never done anything a week in advance in my entire life."

"What was that photography project you stayed up all night finishing the day it was due?" Kendra reminded her.

"Okay, but that turned out amazing," Destiny protested. "I work well under pressure."

"So do they," Maya pointed at the calculation sheets. "But they've been under pressure every day of their professional lives. Not just deadline pressure, but the pressure of being the first, of knowing if they fail, it hurts every Black woman who comes after them."

This sobered them all. The weight of representation, of being a "first," was something they understood all too well, even in their own time. How much heavier that burden must have been in 1956, when so many doors remained firmly closed to Black women.

"I wonder if they knew," Destiny said quietly. "If they had any idea how important their work would be, not just for the space program but for... well, for girls like us."

"Probably not," Kendra replied. "They were just doing their jobs, using their talents, fighting for opportunities. The impact of that ripples forward in ways they couldn't have imagined."

The familiar tingling sensation began at the base of Maya's spine. "I think we're moving again," she warned, reaching for her friends' hands.

"Already?" Destiny complained. "We barely got to talk to them."

"Maybe that was the point," Maya suggested as the office around them began to blur. "Just to recognize them, to acknowledge their contribution when so few people did at the time."

"To witness another kind of courage," Kendra said thoughtfully. "Not marching or protesting, but showing up day after day, calculating launch trajectories in a segregated office, fighting for education and opportunity through excellence."

"And to remind me why I should appreciate my calculator app more," Destiny added, though her usual humor was tempered with genuine respect. "I'm going to think of Mary Jackson next time I complain about math homework."

"That'll last about five minutes," Kendra teased.

"Hey, personal growth happens in small steps," Destiny shot back with a grin.

As the world dissolved around them, Maya's last thought was that history was made in many ways—not just in dramatic confrontations and speeches, but in offices like this one, where Black women bent over calculation sheets and quietly changed the course of the space race, and with it, the world.

The pull of time was gentler now, almost comfortable in its familiarity. They had no way of knowing where—when—they would land next, but Maya found herself looking forward to it, curious rather than anxious about what historical moment the book would reveal to them next.

For now, though, she carried the image of Mary Jackson and Dorothy Vaughan with her through the swirling vortex of time—brilliant minds working in quiet dedication, calculating the paths that would eventually lead humanity to the stars. Not just making history, but making the future possible, one equation at a time.

Chapter 12
Before Rosa

The sensation of traveling through time had become almost familiar—the swirling colors, the weightless floating, the gentle tug as reality reassembled itself around them. This time, when the world solidified, they found themselves standing at a bus stop, the afternoon sun beating down with unexpected intensity.

"Please let this be somewhere with air conditioning," Destiny groaned, immediately fanning herself with her hand. "Preferably sometime after the invention of iced coffee."

Maya glanced around, taking in their surroundings. They were on a city street lined with small business-es—a pharmacy, a five-and-dime store, a barbershop with a striped pole spinning lazily in the heat. Cars rumbled past, their designs suggesting the 1950s again, though different from the ones they'd seen in the NASA parking lot. The street signs read "Montgomery" and "Court Square."

"We're in Montgomery, Alabama," she announced. "And judging by the cars and clothes, we're still in the 1950s."

Kendra, always attentive to details, was the first to notice their outfits had changed again. "Look at our clothes," she said, examining her simple cotton dress with a peter pan collar. "We're dressed like students."

They were indeed—all three wore modest dresses that hit well below the knee, white ankle socks, and sensible shoes. Their hair was styled simply, with Destiny's pulled back in a ponytail, Kendra's in a neat bob, and Maya's in carefully pressed curls. They each carried schoolbooks and small purses.

"School uniforms?" Destiny grimaced, tugging at her collar. "The book has a sick sense of humor."

"Not uniforms," Maya corrected her. "Just standard clothes for Black teenage girls in the South during this era. Conservative, proper, nothing that would draw attention."

"Well, it's hot and itchy and I hate it," Destiny complained, shifting uncomfortably. "And these shoes pinch my toes like medieval torture devices. If time travel has taught me anything, it's that historical fashion was created by people who genuinely hated women."

"At least we blend in," Kendra pointed out practically. "No more strange looks for our 'California fashion' or whatever excuse we've been using."

A city bus rumbled toward them, belching gray exhaust as it pulled up to the stop. Several people lined up to board—mostly white passengers who entered through the front door, followed by Black passengers who paid at the front but then exited to re-enter through the back door.

"Oh," Maya said softly as understanding dawned. "I think I know when we are."

"When?" Destiny asked, then followed Maya's gaze to the bus. "Oh. Segregated buses. So we're before—"

"Before Rosa Parks," Kendra finished. "But I'm guessing not much before, if the book's pattern holds."

The three of them joined the line, standing behind an older Black woman balancing grocery bags and a teenage girl about their age. The girl kept checking her watch, her expression suggesting she was running late for something important. She wore a similar outfit to theirs, though her dress was pressed with military precision, and her school-books were wrapped in protective brown paper.

As they shuffled forward in line, Maya studied the girl more carefully. There was something familiar about her—the determined set of her jaw, the intelligence in her eyes, the way she held herself with careful dignity. A suspicion began to form in Maya's mind.

"Excuse me," she said to the girl. "Are you heading to school?"

The girl turned, giving Maya an appraising look before answering. "Just coming from school, actually. Going home now." She spoke carefully, her diction precise and measured.

"Us too," Maya improvised, gesturing to her friends. "We're new in town. I'm Maya, and this is Kendra and Destiny."

"Claudette," the girl replied simply. "Claudette Colvin."

Maya felt her heart skip a beat, and she heard Kendra's sharp intake of breath. Claudette Colvin—the fifteen-year-old girl who had refused to give up her seat on a Montgomery bus nine months before Rosa Parks's more famous protest. The teenager whose act of courage had helped spark the Montgomery Bus Boycott, though history had largely forgotten her name.

"Nice to meet you, Claudette," Maya managed, hoping her voice sounded normal.

The bus doors opened with a hydraulic hiss, and the white passengers boarded first, dropping their dimes in the collection box and taking seats in the front section. Then the Black passengers paid their fares before exiting and walking to the rear door to board from the back.

"I hate this part," Claudette muttered, almost to herself. "Pay the same fare but have to walk around like we're not good enough to use the front door."

"It's ridiculous," Destiny agreed immediately, never one to hold back her opinions. "Complete nonsense."

Claudette gave her a measuring look. "You really are new in town, aren't you? Better be careful who hears you talking like that."

They reached the front of the line. Claudette paid her fare, then stepped back out to walk to the rear door. The three time travelers did the same, fumbling in their purses to find—miraculously—the correct change for the bus. The book's attention to detail was becoming more impressive with each jump.

As they made their way toward the back entrance, Destiny stumbled slightly on her unfamiliar shoes, nearly toppling into a newspaper stand. "Whoever invented these shoes never actually attempted to walk in them," she grumbled. "They were probably the same genius who decided we need to do this ridiculous front-door-pay, back-door-sit dance."

"You talk real different," Claudette observed as they boarded through the rear door. "Where'd you say you're from?"

"Orlando," Maya supplied, sticking with their established backstory. "Our fathers work at the university there."

The bus was surprisingly crowded. The "Colored" section at the back had only a few vacant seats, despite several empty rows in the white section up front. Claudette slid into a seat about halfway back, in the first row of the colored section. Destiny dropped into the seat beside her, while Maya and Kendra took the seat across the aisle.

"So which school do you attend?" Claudette asked as the bus lurched into motion, the engine grumbling beneath them.

"Lincoln," Maya replied, maintaining their cover story. "We just transferred. What about you?"

"Booker T. Washington," Claudette said. "I'm studying hard. Want to be a lawyer someday."

"That's amazing," Kendra said sincerely. "What made you want to study law?"

Claudette's expression grew more animated, her eyes brightening with passion. "I want to fight for our rights. Real equality, not this separate-but-equal nonsense." She lowered her voice. "We've been studying the Constitution in school. It doesn't say anything about treating people differently because of their color. But that's not how they teach it to us."

"How do they teach it?" Destiny asked, genuinely curious.

"Like we should be grateful for what we have," Claudette replied, a hint of fire in her eyes. "Like asking for actual equality is asking for too much."

Maya felt a chill despite the bus's stifling heat. She knew what was coming—what was going to happen on this very bus ride. Claudette Colvin, exactly their age, was about to make history, and they were sitting right beside her.

The bus continued its route, stopping every few blocks to let passengers on and off. The hydraulic brakes squealed at each stop, and the smell of exhaust occasionally wafted through the open windows. At one stop, several white passengers boarded, filling most of the designated white section. As the bus started moving again, the driver kept glancing in his rearview mirror at the seating arrangement.

"You know," Destiny said quietly to Claudette, "someday things will be different. All this segregation nonsense will be illegal."

"I know," Claudette replied with surprising certainty. "That's what we're fighting for. My teacher, Mrs. Nesbitt, she's been teaching us about civil disobedience and our constitutional rights."

Maya caught Kendra's eye. The dramatic irony was almost unbearable—Claudette had no idea that in minutes, she would put those lessons to the ultimate test, becoming part of a historical moment that would help launch the modern Civil Rights Movement.

At the next stop, more white passengers got on, and now all the seats in the white section were taken. A middle-aged white woman remained standing, looking pointedly at the Black section, her lips pursed in entitled expectation.

The driver called back, "I need those seats," indicating the first row of the colored section—the row where Claudette and Destiny were sitting.

Two Black women across from them immediately stood and moved further back. But Claudette remained seated, her back stiffening visibly. Beside her, Destiny looked to Maya with wide, questioning eyes.

"You too, girl," the driver said more forcefully, glaring at Claudette in the rearview mirror. "Move to the back."

"I paid my fare," Claudette replied, her voice steady but tight with emotion. "I don't have to move."

The bus went silent. Every passenger seemed to freeze, the only sound the rumbling of the engine as the driver pulled over to the curb. The air inside the bus felt suddenly electric, charged with tension and possibility.

"I said move to the back," he repeated, standing now and turning to face them. "That's the law."

"It's against the law to arrest someone who hasn't done anything wrong," Claudette responded, the tremor in her voice betraying her fear despite her brave words.

Maya could hardly breathe. This was it—the moment of defiance that should have been remembered as the spark of the Montgomery Bus Boycott, but instead became a historical footnote.

Destiny still hadn't moved, seemingly rooted in place beside Claudette. Maya caught her eye, giving her a small nod. Whatever happened next, they would follow Claudette's lead.

The driver's face flushed with anger, a vein pulsing visibly at his temple. "I'm calling the police," he threatened, his Southern drawl thickening with rage. "Last chance."

"I know my constitutional rights," Claudette replied, clutching her schoolbooks tighter, knuckles white with tension.

"You're gonna know jail is what you're gonna know," the driver snapped, storming off the bus, presumably to find a police call box.

In the tense silence that followed, punctuated only by nervous whispers and the idling engine, Claudette turned to Destiny. "You should move," she said quietly. "No sense in both of us getting arrested."

"I'm staying right here," Destiny said firmly. "If you're not moving, I'm not moving."

Maya and Kendra exchanged alarmed glances. This wasn't in the history books—Claudette Colvin had been alone in her protest. Destiny was changing history.

"Destiny," Maya hissed across the aisle. "I don't think—"

"I'm not leaving her alone," Destiny whispered back fiercely. "History might have forgotten her, but I won't."

Before Maya could respond, two police officers boarded the bus, nightsticks in hand, their heavy footsteps echoing in the silent vehicle. They approached Claudette and Destiny with unmistakable menace, their faces set in stern disapproval.

"You girls refusing to give up your seats?" one officer demanded, hand resting on his nightstick.

"I paid my fare," Claudette repeated, her voice smaller now but still determined. "I have a right to sit here."

"You have a right to do what the law says," the officer retorted. "And the law says coloreds move back when seats are needed."

"Actually, sir," Kendra spoke up suddenly, "the Fourteenth Amendment guarantees equal protection under the law to all citizens, regardless of race."

The officer turned his glare on her. "You want to be arrested too, smart mouth?"

Maya realized with growing alarm that this situation was spiraling out of control. They weren't supposed to be part of this historical moment—they were supposed to be witnessing it, not changing it. If they got arrested alongside Claudette Colvin, who knew how it might alter the timeline?

"We're not looking for trouble, officer," she said quickly. "We're new in town and didn't understand the rules."

"Well, understand them now," the officer growled. "Get to the back of the bus."

Maya stood, pulling Kendra up with her. "Come on, Destiny," she said pointedly. "Let's move."

Destiny remained stubbornly seated beside Claudette, who looked increasingly nervous as the situation escalated.

"Last chance," the officer said, his hand tightening on his nightstick.

"Destiny," Maya pleaded. "Please."

With visible reluctance, Destiny finally stood. "This isn't right," she said, loud enough for the entire bus to hear. "And someday everyone will know it."

The officers turned their attention solely to Claudette now, who still hadn't moved.

"Are you getting up, or are you getting arrested?" one demanded.

Claudette lifted her chin. "You have no right to do this."

What happened next was a blur of motion and shouts. The officers roughly pulled Claudette from her seat, one grabbing each arm. She didn't resist physically but continued to protest verbally as they handcuffed her.

"I paid my fare! I have rights! This is segregation, and it's against my constitutional rights!"

As they dragged her toward the front of the bus, she called out, "Call my mother! Tell her I've been arrested!"

Then she was gone, escorted off the bus and into a waiting police car. The bus remained stopped, the passengers sitting in stunned silence. A baby started crying somewhere in the back, the sound piercing the heavy quiet.

Maya pulled her friends to the very back row, where they huddled together, whispering urgently.

"I can't believe they just arrested her," Destiny fumed, hands shaking with anger. "She's fifteen! She's our age! All she did was refuse to move."

"That's how it happened historically," Maya confirmed. "Claudette Colvin was arrested, taken to jail, fingerprinted, and charged with violating segregation laws, disturbing the peace, and assaulting an officer."

"Assaulting?" Kendra repeated incredulously. "She didn't touch anyone!"

"They claimed she kicked and fought when they removed her from the bus," Maya explained. "It's their word against hers, and in 1955 Alabama..."

"A Black girl's word means nothing," Destiny finished bitterly. "Some things never change."

"But things do change," Maya insisted. "What Claudette did today—March 2, 1955—it matters. It's one of the catalysts for the Montgomery Bus Boycott that starts later this year. Her arrest gets attention, gets people talking."

"But nobody remembers her," Destiny argued. "Everyone knows Rosa Parks, but Claudette Colvin? I'd never heard of her until that special report we watched in Ms. Washington's class."

"I wonder why they didn't use her case instead of waiting for Rosa Parks," Kendra mused. "She was so young, so brave. It would have been powerful."

"The movement leaders decided Claudette wasn't the right... image," Maya explained carefully. "Rosa Parks was older, had a steady job as a seamstress, was active in the NAACP. They were strategic about who would be the face of the movement."

"Strategic activism," Kendra noted. "They were planning their protests carefully, choosing the perfect test cases."

"And a teenager wasn't perfect enough?" Destiny scoffed.

"It was more complicated than that," Maya said. "There were concerns about how the press would portray her, whether she could withstand the pressure and scrutiny. They needed someone whose reputation was unassailable."

"But she's our age," Destiny insisted. "Fifteen. And she just did something braver than anything I've ever done. We should remember her name alongside Rosa Parks."

"We do remember her now," Maya said. "That's why we're here. To witness her courage, to know her story. To see that people our age can change history."

The bus eventually resumed its route, the atmosphere thick with tension. No one spoke above a whisper. The white woman who'd remained standing rather than take Claudette's seat now sat stiffly, studiously avoiding eye contact with anyone.

"My feet hurt and my dress is itchy, but I'm not complaining about these ridiculous shoes anymore," Destiny said quietly. "Not after watching that."

"I wanted to say something," Kendra admitted. "Do something more. But..."

"But we can't change history," Maya finished for her. "We've tried before. The book seems to prevent it somehow."

"Still," Destiny said, "I wish I'd stayed seated with her. So she wasn't alone."

"You were willing to," Maya pointed out. "That counts for something."

The bus reached another stop, and most of the passengers hurried off, eager to escape the tense atmosphere. The three girls remained seated, uncertain what to do next.

"Do we just... get off at some random stop?" Kendra asked. "We don't exactly have a destination here."

"I guess we—" Maya began, but stopped as the familiar tingling sensation started at the base of her spine. "Actually, I think we're moving on."

"Good timing," Destiny muttered, reaching for her friends' hands. "I've had enough of 1955 Montgomery public transit for one day."

As the bus around them began to fade, its edges blurring into indistinct shapes, Maya found herself thinking about Claudette Colvin—fifteen years old, the same age as they were, standing up for her rights against impossible odds. If a girl their age could help spark a movement that would change America forever, what might they be capable of when they returned to their own time?

The last thing she saw before the bus dissolved completely was a newspaper someone had left on the seat—the Montgomery Advertiser, dated March 2, 1955. Tomorrow's headline would mention a "juvenile Negro girl" arrested for defying bus segregation laws. Most readers would barely notice it. None would guess how that small act of defiance by a teenage girl would help set in motion events that would eventually dismantle Jim Crow.

As they fell through time once more, Maya wondered what other forgotten heroes they might meet—and what courage they might find in themselves along the way.

Chapter 13
A Mother's Courage

The first thing Maya noticed when the world stopped spinning was the overwhelming heat. Not the moderate warmth of Montgomery or the stifling stuffiness of the bus, but true, oppressive heat that pressed down like a physical weight. The kind of heat that made breathing feel like work.

"Is it possible to die of heat stroke in the past?" Destiny gasped, dramatically fanning herself. "Because I think I'm about to become the first recorded case."

They stood on the edges of a massive crowd gathered in what appeared to be a public park. Hundreds of people—mostly Black, though Maya spotted some white faces scattered throughout—filled a grassy expanse before a simple wooden stage. Everyone was dressed in their Sunday best despite the sweltering temperature: men in suits and ties, women in dresses and gloves, children fidgeting in stiff collars and polished shoes.

"Where are we now?" Kendra asked, squinting against the bright sunlight.

Maya turned in a slow circle, taking in their surroundings. The crowd. The makeshift stage. The atmosphere of anticipation. And their own clothing, which had changed once again—similar to their 1950s Montgomery outfits but slightly more formal, as if dressed for church.

Unlike in Montgomery, however, their hairstyles had remained distinctly themselves. Maya's box braids were neatly arranged, adorned with small wooden beads that clicked softly when she moved her head. Kendra's natural curls were shaped into a precise bob that somehow worked with the period clothing, and Destiny's hair was pulled back with a scarf that matched her dress.

"I think the book is fine-tuning our appearances," Maya observed. "Changing our clothes to help us blend in, but keeping our personal styles."

"Thank goodness," Destiny said, touching her styled edges with relief. "I don't think I could handle whatever 'historically accurate' hairstyle they'd have given me. No offense to our ancestors, but some of those styles were criminal."

A murmur rippled through the crowd, drawing their attention back to the stage where a man had stepped up to a microphone. He appeared to be introducing someone, though they were too far away to hear his words clearly.

"Let's get closer," Maya suggested, already edging forward through the crowd.

They carefully navigated their way toward the stage, apologizing as they squeezed between families and couples. The crowd was dense but not hostile to their movement—an atmosphere of shared purpose seemed to unite everyone, creating a sense of community despite the uncomfortable heat.

"I still don't know where—when—we are," Kendra whispered as they found a spot with a better view. "1950s or 60s, obviously, but which moment?"

Before Maya could hazard a guess, a woman approached the microphone. She was in her forties, dressed simply but elegantly in a blue dress, her bearing dignified and composed. There was something familiar about her, though Maya couldn't immediately place her.

"Thank you all for coming today," the woman began, her voice clear and measured. "Though I wish it were under different circumstances."

A hush fell over the crowd. Even the children seemed to sense the importance of the moment, their usual restlessness temporarily stilled.

"Two days ago, they murdered my son," the woman continued, her composure remarkable given her words. "They beat him, they mutilated him, and they threw his body in the Tallahatchie River."

Maya felt her blood run cold despite the heat. Beside her, Kendra gasped softly, and Destiny reached instinctively for both their hands.

"Emmett Till's mother," Maya whispered, recognition dawning. "Mamie Till-Mobley. This is her speaking about her decision to have an open casket for her son."

The woman—Mamie—continued, her voice never breaking though the pain behind her words was palpable. "I wanted the world to see what they did to my boy. I wanted everyone to see because there comes a time when people get tired of being pushed around."

"September 1955," Kendra murmured. "Just months after Claudette Colvin."

"The book is connecting these moments," Maya realized. "Showing us how they built on each other."

Mamie Till-Mobley spoke for perhaps ten minutes, describing her son, the trip to visit family in Mississippi that had ended in his lynching, and her decision to hold an open-casket funeral. Her words were measured but powerful, devoid of self-pity yet devastating in their clarity.

"They didn't just kill Emmett," she said toward the end of her speech. "They killed generations of Black men and women who might have come from him. They killed dreams. They killed hope. But they also woke something up in every mother, every father, every child who saw what they did. They woke up a determination that this must end."

The crowd responded with murmurs of agreement, some crying openly, others nodding with grim determination. An older woman near Maya dabbed at her eyes with a handkerchief, while a father lifted his young son onto his shoulders, as if ensuring the child would remember this moment.

"I don't think I could be that strong," Destiny whispered, tears streaming down her face. "If that was my child..."

"She turned her grief into purpose," Kendra said softly. "Into a catalyst for change."

Maya couldn't speak, her throat tight with emotion. They had already encountered Emmett Till in their journey—had tried, futilely, to warn him away from Mississippi. Seeing his mother now, witnessing her transform her unimaginable loss into a rallying cry for justice, was almost unbearable.

As Mamie finished speaking, a gospel choir took the stage, their harmonies swelling in a hymn of mourning and resilience. The crowd joined in, hundreds of voices rising together in shared grief and determination.

"Amazing grace, how sweet the sound, that saved a wretch like me..."

The song washed over them, powerful in its simplicity, a thread connecting generations of struggle and hope. A slight breeze finally stirred the oppressive air, bringing momentary relief as it carried the music across the gathering.

"I once was lost, but now am found, was blind, but now I see..."

A woman standing next to them noticed Destiny's tears and wordlessly offered her a handkerchief. Destiny accepted with a grateful nod, dabbing at her eyes.

"You girls came all the way from Chicago?" the woman asked, mistaking their emotional response for a personal connection to the family.

"No, ma'am," Maya replied. "We're just... here to bear witness."

The woman nodded as if this made perfect sense. "That's what we all must do now. Witness. Remember. And then act."

As the choir continued, another figure approached the microphone—a young minister with a compelling presence despite his youth. Maya recognized him instantly: Martin Luther King Jr., still in his twenties, not yet the iconic figure he would become but already emerging as a voice for the movement.

"We gather today not only to mourn a child taken too soon," he began, his resonant voice capturing the crowd's attention immediately, "but to commit ourselves to ensuring his death serves as a turning point in our long struggle for justice."

His words were powerful but not yet polished into the soaring rhetoric he would later be known for. This was Dr. King still developing his voice, honing the skills that would eventually move millions. Still, the natural charisma and moral clarity that would define his leadership were already evident.

"This young boy's death must be a catalyst," he continued. "A catalyst for what? For renewed commitment to the cause of justice. For unwavering dedication to the fight for true equality. For the courage to stand up and say 'No more.'"

The crowd responded with increasing enthusiasm, calls of "Yes!" and "Tell it!" punctuating his speech. An elderly man near them nodded vigorously at each point, occasionally raising his hand in agreement.

Maya found herself mesmerized, watching history unfold before her eyes—the convergence of Emmett Till's murder, his mother's brave decision, and the rising voice of Dr. King all combining to accelerate the civil rights movement.

"Is it weird that I keep thinking about Claudette?" Destiny whispered. "How she was basically our age, and Emmett was even younger, and they both changed history just by existing and standing up for themselves?"

"Not weird at all," Kendra replied. "That's exactly what we should be thinking about."

"Young people have always been at the center of movements for change," Maya added. "Sometimes by choice, sometimes by circumstance."

As Dr. King's speech built to its conclusion, calling for peaceful resistance in the face of violence and legal action against Till's murderers, the crowd's energy transformed. What had begun as a gathering of mourning was ending as a rally for action—faces that had been tear-streaked now showed determination; shoulders that had been slumped with grief now straightened with purpose.

"That's masterful," Kendra observed quietly. "How he's channeling their pain into resolve."

"It's what great leaders do," Maya agreed. "They don't just speak to people's emotions; they transform them."

"I'd settle for someone transforming this heat," Destiny muttered, though her attempt at humor was halfhearted. The day's emotional weight had clearly affected her deeply.

As Dr. King concluded his remarks, the crowd began to disperse slowly, breaking into small groups that lingered to discuss what they'd heard. The atmosphere had shifted perceptibly—from collective grief to collective determination.

"I wish we could have known Emmett," Destiny said suddenly as they stood watching people depart. "Not just tried to warn him in that moment, but really known him. What his laugh sounded like. What made him happy. Who he might have become."

"That's what makes his murder so devastating," Kendra replied. "All that potential, all that future, stolen."

"But look at what his mother did with her grief," Maya pointed out, nodding toward the stage where Mamie Till-Mobley was now speaking quietly with several community leaders. "She could have mourned privately, processed her loss away from public view. Instead, she forced America to look at what had been done to her son."

"The courage that took..." Destiny shook her head in wonder. "I can't even imagine."

As they watched, Mamie happened to glance in their direction. For a brief moment, their eyes met across the distance—three teenage girls from the future and a mother whose courage would help change the course of history. Something in her expression shifted, a flicker of recognition perhaps, though Maya knew that was impossible.

The moment was broken when someone approached Mamie with a question, turning her attention away. But that brief connection lingered with Maya, a reminder that they weren't just passive observers in these historical moments—somehow, in ways they didn't fully understand, they were present in them.

"I think it's time to go," she said to her friends. "We've seen what we needed to see here."

As if responding to her words, the familiar tingling sensation began at the base of her spine. "Right on cue," she added with a small smile. "The book agrees."

"Where do you think we're going next?" Kendra asked as they linked hands, preparing for the transition.

"I don't know," Maya admitted. "But I'm starting to trust the book's purpose. Each jump seems connected to the others, building a narrative of struggle and progress."

"As long as the next place has air conditioning," Destiny said, managing a weak smile despite her tear-streaked face. "I've sweat through historical outfits in two different decades now."

The tingling intensified, spreading from Maya's spine to her fingertips. The world around them began to blur—the park, the stage, the dispersing crowd all dissolving into indistinct shapes and colors.

The last thing Maya saw before everything disappeared completely was Mamie Till-Mobley's face—composed, dignified, and utterly determined. The face of a woman who had transformed unbearable personal tragedy into a force for collective change. The face of courage in its purest form.

And then they were falling once more, three friends linked by clasped hands and shared experiences, tumbling through the corridors of time toward their next destination.

Chapter 14

By the Stroke of a Pen

The landing was gentler this time, as if they were getting better at this time-traveling business. When reality reassembled itself around them, they found themselves standing in the back of a crowded auditorium. Unlike the open-air gathering they'd just left, this was a formal indoor venue—wood-paneled walls, rows of seats filled with attentive listeners, a proper stage with a podium bearing an official-looking seal.

"Air conditioning," Destiny sighed with palpable relief, closing her eyes to savor the cool air. "Whoever invented this deserves a national holiday."

"Willis Carrier, 1902," Maya supplied automatically, then shrugged when her friends gave her amused looks.

"What? My dad's lectures cover all kinds of random historical facts."

"Where are we?" Kendra asked, scanning their surroundings with her usual attention to detail. "When are we?"

Maya studied the room, taking in the crowd, the formal
atmosphere, the sense of anticipation. Their clothing had
changed again—more refined now, suits and dresses in the
style of the early 1960s. Maya's box braids were styled into
an elegant updo, while Kendra and Destiny's hair was similarly formal.

At the podium stood a man she recognized from history
books and documentaries—President Lyndon B. Johnson,
looking solemn in a dark suit as he addressed the assembled
crowd.

"We're at the signing of the Civil Rights Act," she realized, excitement building in her chest. "July 2, 1964."

"No way," Destiny breathed, her earlier emotion giving
way to awe. "The actual signing? Like, the law that made
segregation illegal?"

"The very one," Maya confirmed, pointing discreetly
toward the front row where several well-dressed Black
men and women sat alongside white civil rights leaders.
"Look—that's Dr. King right there. And Roy Wilkins from

the NAACP. And I think that's Rosa Parks a few seats over."

"It is," Kendra confirmed, her artist's eye picking out the woman's distinct profile. "She looks so small in person. Almost fragile. But we know better."

President Johnson was speaking, his Texas drawl carrying clearly through the room: "We believe that all men are created equal. Yet many are denied equal treatment. We believe that all men have certain unalienable rights. Yet many Americans do not enjoy those rights..."

"From Claudette Colvin to the Civil Rights Act," Kendra murmured, her voice tinged with wonder. "Less than a decade of struggle and sacrifice to change laws that had stood for generations."

"Notice who's not here though," Maya said quietly. "Claudette Colvin. Mamie Till-Mobley. All the everyday people whose courage and loss paved the way for this moment."

"The forgotten catalysts," Destiny said, surprising her friends with the poetic phrasing. When they looked at her, she shrugged. "What? I pay attention sometimes. My poetry slam phase wasn't entirely wasted."

"You had a poetry slam phase?" Kendra asked, momentarily distracted. "How did I not know this?"

"There are depths to me, Mitchell," Destiny replied with exaggerated dignity. "Mysterious, poetic depths."

Maya suppressed a laugh, grateful for the moment of levity amid the weight of history. This was one of the things she loved most about her friends—their ability to find humor even in the most serious situations, to keep each other grounded when everything around them was extraordinary.

They listened as Johnson continued his address, speaking about the moral imperative of equality and the work still to be done. The room was tense with the weight of history—some faces shining with triumph, others tight with barely concealed resistance to the changes being enacted.

"It's strange," Kendra observed, "seeing the moment of victory after witnessing so much of the struggle. It feels..."

"Incomplete," Maya supplied. "Because we know the law didn't instantly change people's hearts or daily realities."

"But it was still a massive victory," Destiny insisted. "Like, we just saw Claudette Colvin get arrested for sitting on a bus, and now we're watching them make that illegal. That's huge."

An elderly Black man standing near them turned and noticed their presence. He studied them curiously, taking in their youthful faces and solemn expressions. His suit was worn but meticulously pressed, and a small pin on his lapel identified him as a member of the NAACP.

"First time in Washington?" he asked kindly.

"Yes, sir," Maya replied, which wasn't entirely a lie.

He nodded, his eyes crinkling at the corners. "Remember this day. Tell your children about it someday. We've been working toward this moment since before you were born."

"We will, sir," Kendra assured him sincerely.

The man smiled. "Good. Too many young people don't understand how hard-won these victories are. How many people sacrificed for this day."

"We've been learning about that," Maya said, thinking of all they had witnessed on their journey. "About Claudette Colvin and Emmett Till and all the others who helped make this possible."

"Claudette Colvin?" The man's eyebrows rose in surprise. "Not many people remember her name. That's good, knowing your history."

"She was our age," Destiny pointed out. "Fifteen. Standing up to segregation while I can barely stand up to my mom about curfew."

The man chuckled. "Youth has always been the engine of change. The elders may guide, but it's the young who push hardest, who imagine what others call impossible." He glanced toward the front of the room. "Even Dr. King was just a young minister when he took on Montgomery."

At the podium, Johnson picked up a pen—the first of many he would use to sign the historic legislation, each to be given as a souvenir to the civil rights leaders present.

"This Civil Rights Act is a challenge to all of us," he said, "to go to work in our communities and our states, in our homes and in our hearts, to eliminate the last vestiges of injustice in our beloved country."

As he bent to sign the document, a hush fell over the crowd. The scratching of the pen against paper was barely audible, yet it seemed to fill the entire room—a simple sound representing the culmination of years of struggle, sacrifice, and perseverance.

"With a stroke of a pen," Kendra whispered, "changing the legal reality for millions of people."

"That's the power of law," Maya agreed. "Though enforcing it will be another battle."

Johnson signed with multiple pens, passing each one to a different civil rights leader. The room erupted in applause when he finished. Many people were crying openly—tears of joy, of relief, of vindication after years of fighting. The civil rights leaders in the front row embraced each other, their usual composure momentarily abandoned in celebration.

"It's beautiful," Kendra said softly. "But also bittersweet, knowing how much was sacrificed to get here. How many people didn't live to see this day."

"And how much work was still ahead," Maya added, thinking of the ongoing struggles that would follow the legislation—the battles for implementation, the white backlash, the assassinations still to come.

The ceremony concluded, and people began filing out of the auditorium, their conversations animated with excitement and speculation about what the new law would mean in practice. The three girls remained in place, unsure what to do next.

"So... what now?" Destiny asked as the room gradually emptied. "Do we just hang around 1964 until the book decides we've seen enough? Because I wouldn't mind getting a closer look at those incredible suits the Freedom Riders are wearing. The tailoring is immaculate."

"Always thinking about fashion," Kendra teased.

"Fashion is political," Destiny replied with unexpected seriousness. "Those perfectly pressed suits and dresses were armor. Respectability as both shield and weapon."

Maya and Kendra stared at her in surprise.

"What?" Destiny defended herself. "I told you I had depths."

As they debated their next move, they noticed a woman approaching them—elegant in a tailored suit, her eyes sharp with intelligence and curiosity. It took Maya a moment to recognize her: Dorothy Height, president of the National Council of Negro Women and a crucial, if often over-looked, figure in civil rights leadership.

"Excuse me, young ladies," she said when she reached them. "I couldn't help noticing you during the ceremony. You seemed... particularly moved."

"Yes, ma'am," Kendra replied. "It's an honor to be here for such a historic moment."

Dorothy Height studied them thoughtfully. "You re-mind me of some of our younger activists. There's a cer tain... awareness in your eyes. A perception beyond your years." She smiled slightly. "Am I correct in assuming you're involved in the movement?"

The girls exchanged glances, uncertain how to respond. In a way, they were involved in the movement—just not in the way Dorothy Height might imagine.

"We're... learning," Maya said finally. "Trying to understand our history and our place in it."

This seemed to satisfy Height. "Good. That's where it starts. Understanding." She reached into her handbag and extracted three small pins—simple blue buttons bearing the letters "NCNW" for her organization. "Here. A small memento of this day."

"Thank you," Maya said, accepting the pin with reverence. This was more than a souvenir; it was a tangible connection to history, to this moment, to the woman standing before them.

"The work doesn't end with this signing," Height told them, her expression growing serious. "In some ways, it only begins. We still have mountains to climb—poverty, education, housing, employment. And we'll need young women like you to lead the way."

"We'll try to be worthy of that responsibility," Kendra replied with genuine feeling.

Height nodded, seemingly satisfied with what she saw in them. "I believe you will." She glanced toward the exit, where a group appeared to be waiting for her. "I must go now. Remember—you're not just witnessing history. You're part of it."

As she walked away, Destiny let out a breath she seemed to have been holding. "Okay, that was intense. Did Dorothy Height just recruit us into the civil rights movement? Because I'm pretty sure that's what just happened."

"In a way," Maya agreed, carefully pinning the NCNW button to her dress. It felt strangely significant, this physical object crossing time with them.

"Wait," Kendra said suddenly, her eyes widening. "Did you feel that?"

The tingling sensation had finally begun, subtle at first but quickly intensifying.

"Here we go again," Destiny said, reaching for their hands. "I wonder where—when—we're going next."

"Somewhere related to this moment, I'd guess," Maya replied as the room began to blur around them. "The book seems to be connecting these events, showing us the through-line of history."

"I'm holding onto my pin," Destiny declared firmly. "First physical evidence of our wild time-traveling adventure."

"Me too," Kendra agreed. "A reminder that we were really there."

The tingling spread from Maya's spine to her fingertips, the world dissolving into swirling colors and fragmented sounds. The last thing she saw before reality fully disintegrated was the simple wooden podium where the Civil Rights Act had been signed—a humble piece of furniture that had just witnessed the legal dismantling of Jim Crow.

And then they were falling again, three friends linked by clasped hands and shared experiences, traveling through the corridors of time toward their next destination. But this time, they carried something with them—three small blue pins, physical reminders that they were not just witnesses to history, but connected to it in ways they were only beginning to understand.

Chapter 15

Standing in the Schoolhouse Door

The landing this time felt like stepping from one room into another—a gentle transition rather than the disorienting tumble they'd grown accustomed to. When the world solidified around them, they found themselves standing on a college campus, massive brick buildings rising around a central quadrangle where a curious scene was unfolding.

A crowd had gathered before the entrance to one of the buildings—students, reporters with bulky cameras and notepads, and what appeared to be National Guardsmen in uniform. The mood was tense, expectant, as if everyone was waiting for something momentous to occur.

"Where are we now?" Kendra asked, her artist's eye already taking in details—the classical architecture of the buildings, the 1960s clothing and hairstyles of the onlookers, the news cameras positioned strategically around the quadrangle.

Maya scanned their surroundings, noting an archway with "University of Alabama" engraved above it. Their own clothing had changed again—simpler than at the Civil Rights Act signing but still neat and respectable: modest dresses, sensible shoes, and, Maya was pleased to note, their own natural hairstyles maintained. Her box braids were arranged in a simple style, the wooden beads still present but less prominent, more appropriate for a daytime setting.

"We're at the University of Alabama," she realized. "And judging by the National Guard presence and all these reporters, I think this is Governor George Wallace's 'stand in the schoolhouse door.'"

"His what now?" Destiny asked, adjusting the NCNW pin she'd somehow managed to keep through their time jump, now attached to her collar.

"June 11, 1963," Maya explained. "When Governor Wallace physically blocked the entrance to prevent the university's first Black students from registering."

Destiny's expression darkened. "Oh great, more racism. Just what I wanted to see after experiencing segregated buses and Emmett Till's murder."

"But this time," Kendra pointed out, "it ends differently. If this is what I think it is, Wallace eventually steps aside. The students register successfully."

"Small victories," Destiny muttered, though her tone lacked real bitterness. They'd witnessed enough history now to understand that progress, however slow and incomplete, was still progress.

The crowd around them shifted, voices rising as a car approached the building. From it emerged two well-dressed Black students—a young man and woman, their expressions composed despite the obvious tension.

"Vivian Malone and James Hood," Maya identified them quietly. "The two students attempting to register."

Behind them came several men in suits—federal officials, Maya guessed, there to ensure the integration proceeded as ordered by the courts.

"Where's the governor?" Kendra asked, scanning the scene.

As if on cue, a stocky man with a determined expression strode into view, positioning himself directly in the doorway of the building. Even at a distance, his body language communicated defiance.

"That's him," Maya confirmed. "George Wallace."

"He looks so... ordinary," Destiny observed. "Like someone's grumpy uncle, not a villain from a history book."

"That's the thing about racists," Kendra said softly. "They don't always look like monsters. Sometimes they look like politicians or teachers or the nice lady down the street."

One of the federal officials approached Wallace, apparently asking him to step aside. Though they couldn't hear the exchange from their position, Wallace's refusal was obvious.

The crowd around them murmured, some with approval, others with dismay. The girls noticed they were getting curious glances from nearby onlookers—three Black teenage girls weren't common sights at integration standoffs.

"Let's move closer," Maya suggested. "I want to hear what they're saying."

They carefully navigated through the crowd, drawing more looks but no direct confrontation. As they got closer to the building entrance, they could finally make out the words being exchanged.

"—the unwelcomed, unwanted, unwarranted and force-induced intrusion upon the campus of the University of Alabama," Wallace was declaring in a practiced speech, his Southern accent thick with indignation. "I stand before you today in place of thousands of other Alabamians whose presence would have confronted you had I been derelict in my duty to them."

"He's playing to the cameras," Kendra observed quietly. "Making sure his supporters see him 'defending' segregation."

"Political theater at its worst," Maya agreed.

The federal official—who Maya now recognized as Deputy Attorney General Nicholas Katzenbach—was attempting to reason with Wallace, his tone firm but measured.

"Governor, I'm not interested in a show," they heard him say. "These students have a right to be here. They are here under federal court order."

"He doesn't even think they're human," Destiny said, noticing how Wallace refused to acknowledge Malone and Hood, who stood with remarkable dignity throughout the confrontation. "He won't even look at them."

"Dehumanization," Kendra nodded. "It's easier to deny people's rights when you pretend they're not really people."

As the standoff continued, Maya felt a surge of admiration for the two students. Standing quietly but firmly, not engaging with Wallace's theatrics, they embodied a courage that was different from the fiery activism they'd witnessed in other historical moments—quieter, perhaps, but no less powerful.

"I can't imagine how they're feeling right now," Maya said. "Knowing the whole country is watching, that they represent so much more than just themselves."

"The pressure must be incredible," Kendra agreed. "One wrong move, one moment of justified anger or frustration, and critics would use it to discredit the entire movement."

"Yet they're just standing there," Destiny observed with growing respect. "Taking it. Staying dignified when I would've already told Wallace exactly where he could stick his segregation speech."

"Which is precisely why movement leaders carefully selected who would integrate schools and universities," Maya pointed out. "They needed people with extraordinary self-control and dignity."

The confrontation reached its climax when Katzenbach finally stepped away, apparently to call for further instructions from Washington. The crowd's tension was palpable as they waited to see what would happen next.

A young white student standing near them turned and noticed their presence. His expression registered surprise, then curiosity.

"You girls aren't from here," he said. It wasn't a question.

"No," Maya replied simply, offering no further explanation.

"You're with them?" he asked, nodding toward Malone and Hood.

"We're with history," Destiny replied with unexpected eloquence, her hand unconsciously touching the NCNW pin at her collar.

The student looked confused for a moment, then thoughtful. "My roommate says this is all inevitable. That segregation's days are numbered."

"Your roommate's right," Kendra said.

"My father says it'll destroy Alabama," the student continued, his expression troubled. "That mixing the races goes against nature."

Maya studied him, sensing not hostility but genuine con-fusion—a young man caught between the values he'd been raised with and the changing world around him.

"What do you think?" she asked gently.

He hesitated, glancing around as if afraid of being over-heard. "I think... I don't know what to think anymore. But I'm a chemistry major, and in chemistry, mixing things often creates something stronger than its separate parts."

A small smile tugged at Maya's lips. "That's not a bad way to look at it."

"Don't tell my father I said that," the student added quickly before drifting away, lost again in the crowd.

"That was unexpected," Destiny commented. "A glimpse of a mind maybe starting to change?"

"That's how it happens sometimes," Maya replied. "Not in dramatic conversions, but in quiet questions and small realizations."

Their attention was drawn back to the main event as a new flurry of activity erupted around Wallace. Someone had arrived with a message, and after a brief exchange, Wal-lace's demeanor subtly shifted.

"What's happening?" Destiny asked, straining to see.

"I think," Maya said slowly, "President Kennedy just federalized the Alabama National Guard. Which means Wallace is about to lose his standoff."

Sure enough, minutes later, the National Guardsmen approached Wallace. Words were exchanged, and then, with as much dignity as he could muster, Wallace stepped aside from the doorway.

A ripple of reactions moved through the crowd—dismay from segregationists, relief from others, and a collective recognition that they were witnessing a pivotal moment in the integration of American education.

Vivian Malone and James Hood, accompanied by federal officials, walked past Wallace and entered the building. Just like that—no violence, no dramatic confrontation, just two students walking through a door that had previously been closed to people who looked like them.

"That's it?" Destiny sounded almost disappointed. "After all that build-up?"

"That's it," Maya confirmed. "And that's the point. Integration happening not with fiery speeches or dramatic confrontations, but with ordinary actions—students walking into a building to register for classes."

"The mundane face of progress," Kendra observed. "It's not always dramatic."

"Though the lead-up sure was," Destiny noted, watching as Wallace, having made his symbolic stand, now departed with his entourage. "All that posturing just to eventually step aside."

"He knew he would lose," Maya explained. "But he needed his supporters to see him fighting to the last moment. Politics," she added with a slight eye roll.

As the crowd began to disperse, the three girls remained in place, watching as reporters packed up their equipment and onlookers drifted away. The historical moment had concluded, but they found themselves reluctant to leave.

"I wonder what happened to them," Destiny said. "Vivian Malone and James Hood. After this day."

"Vivian Malone became the first Black graduate of the University of Alabama in 1965," Maya supplied. "Hood transferred to another school but eventually returned and earned his doctorate from Alabama in 1997."

"That's a long time between starting and finishing," Kendra observed.

"Sometimes the journey isn't straight," Maya shrugged. "But they both made history just by walking through that door."

They watched as the campus gradually returned to normal, the extraordinary moment fading back into ordinary college life. Students who had gathered to witness the confrontation now headed to libraries or dining halls, the brief interruption to their routine already becoming yesterday's news.

"It's strange," Kendra said thoughtfully, "how quickly the extraordinary becomes ordinary. A few years before this, Black students at the University of Alabama would have been unthinkable. Now it's just... reality."

"That's how change works," Maya replied. "What seems impossible one day becomes inevitable the next, and ordinary the day after that."

"I like that," Destiny said, a rare moment of philosophical appreciation. "The impossible becoming ordinary. Maybe that's what progress really looks like."

As they contemplated this idea, Maya noticed a young Black woman approaching them. She appeared to be a student, carrying books and walking with purpose.

"You three need to be more careful," she said when she reached them, her voice low but urgent. "Standing around staring like that, you're attracting attention."

"Sorry," Maya apologized automatically. "We were just—"

"I know what you were doing," the woman interrupted. "Witnessing. I get it. But this isn't the safest place for us right now." She glanced around nervously. "Some folks aren't happy about today's events."

"We're just leaving," Kendra assured her.

The woman studied them curiously. "You're not from the local high school, are you? I don't recognize you."

"We're visitors," Destiny replied, using their standard explanation.

"Well, visitor or not, be careful. Things are changing, but not everyone's happy about it." She hesitated, then added more softly, "Though I am. My younger sister might be able to apply here next year because of what happened today."

With that, she continued on her way, leaving the girls with a renewed appreciation for the real-world impact of the moment they'd just witnessed—not just as history, but as a door opening for countless individuals in the years to come.

"Ready to move on?" Maya asked her friends, sensing they'd seen what they needed to see here.

As if responding to her question, the familiar tingling sensation began at the base of her spine, spreading outward in gentle waves.

"Perfect timing," Destiny remarked. "Though I wouldn't have minded exploring the campus a bit more. I bet they have a decent cafeteria."

"Always thinking about food," Kendra teased.

"Time travel burns calories!" Destiny protested as the world began to blur around them. "Witnessing historical racism is exhausting work."

Maya laughed despite herself, grateful once again for her friend's ability to find humor even in the strangest circumstances. As the University of Alabama dissolved into swirling colors and indistinct shapes, she found herself wondering what historical moment awaited them next.

Unlike previous jumps, she felt not apprehension but curiosity—a growing sense that each of these moments was connecting to form a larger picture, a tapestry of struggle and progress that had shaped the world they knew. And somehow, in ways she didn't yet fully understand, their own story was becoming interwoven with that history.

The NCNW pin on her dress—a physical object carried through time—seemed proof of this connection. They weren't just witnesses to history; they were, in some small way, participants in it.

As they fell through time once more, three friends linked by clasped hands and shared experiences, Maya felt a growing certainty that their journey was building toward something significant. What that might be, she couldn't yet say—but she was increasingly eager to find out.

Chapter 16
Greenwood's Glory and Grief

The world stabilized around them with unusual gentleness, as if the book itself recognized they needed a moment of reprieve after their previous experiences. Instead of the disorienting tumble, this transition felt more like stepping from one room into another.

They found themselves on a bustling street unlike any they'd visited so far. Well-dressed Black men and women moved purposefully along the sidewalks, entering shops with gleaming display windows and elegant signage. A row of brick buildings housed businesses of every description—a grocery store, a haberdashery, a photographer's studio, several restaurants, and even a movie theater with a brightly painted marquee.

Most striking was the atmosphere—an air of prosperity, dignity, and self-sufficiency that permeated the scene. No signs of segregation, no white faces overseeing the commerce. This was clearly a thriving Black community, operating on its own terms.

"Where are we?" Destiny asked, turning slowly to take it all in. "This doesn't look like any historical moment we've visited before."

Maya examined their surroundings more carefully. Their clothing had changed again—dresses in the fashion of the early 1920s, with dropped waists and hemlines that daringly revealed their ankles. Maya's box braids were tucked beneath a stylish cloche hat, while Kendra and Destiny wore similarly fashionable headwear. All three carried small beaded handbags.

"I think," Maya said slowly, recognition dawning, "we're in Tulsa, Oklahoma. Greenwood District. Sometime around 1921."

"Greenwood?" Destiny repeated, still taking in the vibrant scene. "Wait, isn't that—"

"Black Wall Street," Kendra finished, her artist's eye already capturing details of the architecture, the clothing, the careful presentation of the storefronts. "Before the massacre."

The significance settled over them in layers—the prosperity they were witnessing, and the knowledge of what would soon happen to it. The Tulsa Race Massacre of 1921, when white mobs would destroy this thriving Black community, killing hundreds and burning thirty-five blocks to the ground.

"This is beautiful," Destiny said softly, watching as a well-dressed couple exited a restaurant, laughing together. "Look at all these Black-owned businesses. All these people just... living well."

"Greenwood was exceptional," Maya confirmed. "One of the most prosperous Black communities in America at this time. They called it 'Black Wall Street' because of the concentration of wealth and businesses."

A newspaper boy on the corner called out headlines, waving the latest edition of the Tulsa Star—a Black-owned newspaper, Maya noted. A Model T driven by a young Black man in a sharp suit cruised slowly down the street. From somewhere nearby, jazz music drifted on the afternoon air.

"I can see why the book brought us here," Kendra said thoughtfully. "After showing us so much struggle and resistance, it's showing us what Black excellence looks like when left unhindered."

"But we know what's coming," Destiny reminded them, her expression darkening. "All of this gets destroyed."

"Not just destroyed," Maya added grimly. "Deliberately erased. The massacre wasn't even taught in Oklahoma schools until recently. It was like they tried to pretend this place never existed."

As they stood absorbing the scene, a woman emerged from a nearby grocery store, arms laden with paper bags. Unlike most of the well-dressed pedestrians, she wore a simple work dress and looked harried, as if running late for something important.

"Excuse me," she called, noting their idle stance. "You girls look strong. Could you help me carry these to Dr. Jackson's office? It's just down the block."

Before they could respond, she had already thrust a bag into Destiny's arms, then Maya's. "Thank you, dears. My name's Addie, by the way. I work for Dr. Jackson—only Negro doctor with his own hospital in the whole state, you know."

"No, we didn't know," Kendra replied, accepting the final bag. Unlike their previous hesitation in historical moments, this simple act of helping seemed harmless enough.

"You must be new to Greenwood," Addie continued as she led them down the street. "I know just about everybody around here, and I don't recognize you three."

"Just visiting," Maya said, their standard explanation. "We've heard a lot about Greenwood."

"Well, there's plenty to hear," Addie said proudly. "We've built something special here. Twenty-one restaurants, four hotels, a hospital, a bank, a post office—all Negro-owned. Some folks call it a city within a city."

"It's impressive," Kendra said sincerely.

"Don't see this many successful Black businesses even in our ti—" Destiny caught herself. "Even in the places we're from."

Addie nodded knowingly. "That's why folks keep coming. Word spreads. Here, a Negro can actually build something, own something, pass something down to their children."

They turned a corner onto another thriving street, this one featuring professional offices—doctors, lawyers, accountants, real estate agents. All Black-owned, all clearly prosperous.

"Here we are," Addie announced, stopping before a handsome brick building with "Jackson Surgical Infirmary" etched onto a brass plaque. "You can just bring those to the kitchen in the back."

They followed her through the lobby—surprisingly modern, with electric lights and polished wooden furniture—to a well-equipped kitchen at the rear of the building.

"These are for tonight's community meeting," Addie explained as they set down their bags. "Dr. Jackson hosts the Negro Business League here once a month. Tonight's topic is expansion—whether to invest in more businesses here or start establishing in other neighborhoods."

The dramatic irony of this hit Maya like a physical blow. These business leaders were planning for a future that would be violently stolen from them within days or possibly hours.

"When exactly is this meeting?" she asked, trying to keep her voice casual.

"Tonight, May 31st," Addie replied, already unpacking the groceries.

Maya exchanged alarmed glances with her friends. May 31, 1921. The massacre would begin that very night.

"Thank you for your help, girls," Addie continued, oblivious to their distress. "Are you in town long? Looking for work, perhaps? Greenwood's always hiring—too much opportunity, not enough hands."

"We're just passing through," Kendra replied, her voice tight. "But thank you."

"Well, enjoy your visit," Addie said cheerfully. "Be sure to catch a picture at the Dreamland Theater if you have time. Best Negro-owned movie house in the country."

As they left the building, the girls huddled together on the sidewalk, speaking in urgent whispers.

"We have to warn them," Destiny said immediately. "The massacre starts tonight. We have to tell them."

"You know we can't change history," Maya reminded her, though her own heart ached with the same desire. "We've tried before."

"This is different," Destiny insisted. "This is hundreds of people who are going to die. Thousands who will lose everything. We have to try."

Kendra, who would normally have asked what they should do, instead grew quiet, her expression thoughtful. After a moment, she spoke with unusual decisiveness.

"I think we need to understand why we're here," she said. "The book hasn't brought us to Greenwood just to witness its destruction. It's brought us here before the tragedy, to see what was lost."

"What difference does that make?" Destiny demanded.

"It makes all the difference," Kendra replied with new-found confidence. "We're not here to change what happens, but to remember it. To witness not just the tragedy, but the triumph that existed before it."

Maya studied her friend with surprise and admiration. Kendra had always been the most uncertain of them, the one most likely to defer to Maya's historical knowledge or Destiny's bold declarations. But their journey had changed her, awakened a wisdom and perspective that now emerged when most needed.

"Kendra's right," Maya agreed. "The book has been showing us a pattern—how progress happens, how it's resisted, how it continues despite setbacks. Greenwood is part of that pattern."

"So we just wander around admiring everything, knowing it's all about to burn?" Destiny asked, frustration evident in her voice.

"No," Kendra said gently. "We bear witness. We remember. We learn what Greenwood really was, so we can carry that truth back with us."

Destiny wasn't entirely convinced, but she nodded reluctantly. "Fine. But I hate this part of time travel."

As they continued down the street, Maya noticed a newspaper stand with the Tulsa Tribune displayed. The headline made her stomach clench: "Nab Negro for Attacking Girl in Elevator."

"That's it," she said quietly, pointing to the paper. "That's the spark. A Black shoeshiner named Dick Rowland was accused of assaulting a white elevator operator. The charges were later dropped, but this headline's going to inflame tensions and trigger the massacre."

"One false accusation," Destiny said bitterly. "One inflammatory headline. And all of this—" she gestured around at the thriving community, "—gets destroyed because of it."

"Not just destroyed," Kendra added, her voice uncharacteristically hard. "Deliberately erased from history. My parents grew up in Oklahoma, and neither of them learned about the massacre in school. It was buried, ignored."

They spent the next few hours exploring Greenwood, their hearts growing heavier with each new discovery of what would soon be lost. They passed the Stradford Hotel—the largest Black-owned hotel in the country—and the offices of the Tulsa Star newspaper. They saw the Dreamland Theater with its proud marquee, and Williams Confectionery where fashionably dressed patrons enjoyed ice cream at small tables.

Most poignant were the residential streets just beyond the business district—neat rows of houses ranging from modest bungalows to impressive two-story homes, all meticulously maintained. Children played in yards. Neighbors chatted across fences. An old man rocked on his porch, smoking a pipe and nodding to passersby.

"All of this," Maya said softly. "All these lives, all this prosperity. By tomorrow, most of it will be ashes."

"And the worst part?" Destiny added. "Most Americans don't even know this happened. It's not in our history books."

"That's why we're here," Kendra said with quiet certainty. "To know it. To remember it. To understand that Black excellence has existed throughout our history, even when it was violently suppressed."

They paused at a street corner, watching as Greenwood went about its ordinary business, blissfully unaware of what the night would bring. A group of children ran past, laughing and chasing a rolling hoop. A young couple strolled arm in arm, window shopping. An older woman swept her front steps, exchanging pleasantries with a mail carrier.

"I keep thinking about that community meeting Addie mentioned," Maya said. "All those business leaders gathering to plan Greenwood's future, not knowing they don't have one."

"They have a future through us," Kendra replied. "Through everyone who learns their story and remembers what was built here."

Destiny, who had been uncharacteristically quiet, suddenly straightened her shoulders. "You know what? We should document this. Like, really document it."

"How?" Maya asked. "Our phones don't work here."

"The old-fashioned way," Destiny replied, determination replacing her earlier frustration. "Kendra, you're an artist. You should draw what we're seeing—the buildings, the people, the details. Maya, you know all the history—you should write down names, dates, facts. And I'll—" she hesitated, then smiled. "I'll talk to people. Get their stories."

"Destiny Turner, social butterfly, using her powers for good," Kendra teased, though her eyes reflected approval.

"Hey, I have depths, remember?" Destiny shot back with a hint of her usual humor. "Mysterious, poetic depths."

For the next couple of hours, they did exactly as Destiny suggested. Kendra found a stationery shop where she purchased a sketchbook and pencils, then positioned herself at various vantage points to capture Greenwood's essence. Maya wrote detailed notes about what they were seeing, including names of businesses and their owners, architectural styles, and cultural observations.

And Destiny, true to her word, spoke with anyone willing to chat—shopkeepers, pedestrians, children. She asked about their lives in Greenwood, their businesses, their dreams. People responded to her genuine interest and natural charm, sharing stories and perspectives that would have otherwise been lost to history.

"The lady who runs the hat shop," she reported back after one such conversation, "started with just a sewing machine in her kitchen. Now she has six employees and supplies three stores in other cities. She's saving to send her daughter to college."

Each story added dimension to their understanding, transformed Greenwood from a historical tragedy to a community of individual dreams, ambitions, and achievements.

As evening approached, the street lamps were lit, and Greenwood transformed. The workday businesses began to close, while restaurants and entertainment venues came alive. Music drifted from several establishments. Couples dressed for a night out strolled the sidewalks.

"We should go," Maya said reluctantly, noting the lengthening shadows. "The violence will start after dark. We don't want to be here when it happens."

"How will we leave?" Kendra asked. "The book hasn't given us any sign of moving on yet."

As if responding to her words, the familiar tingling sensation began at the base of Maya's spine. "Ask and you shall receive," she said with a sad smile. "I think it's time."

They found a quiet alley where they could depart unobserved, linking hands as the tingling intensified. The world around them began to blur, Greenwood's vibrant evening fading into indistinct shapes and colors.

"I'm glad we saw it like this," Destiny said, her voice tight with emotion. "Beautiful and thriving. Not just as a victim."

"That's the point, I think," Maya replied as reality continued to dissolve around them. "To know what was built, not just what was destroyed. To understand that the story of Black America isn't just about suffering and resistance, but about achievement and excellence too."

"Even when that excellence was deliberately erased," Kendra added.

The last thing they saw before Greenwood disappeared completely was a family walking down the sidewalk—parents and three children, dressed for an evening out, laughing together. An ordinary moment of joy that, like so much else in Greenwood, would soon be consumed by hatred and violence.

But the girls had seen it. Had documented it. Would remember it. And in that remembering, some small piece of Greenwood's glory would survive its grief.

Then they were falling again, three friends linked by clasped hands and shared experiences, carrying the weight of history's forgotten truths as they tumbled toward whatever moment awaited them next.

Chapter 17

Motown's Moment

The world reassembled around them in a blur of sound and color, but instead of the usual disorienting landing, they found themselves standing in what appeared to be a long hallway. The walls were painted institutional beige, but someone had made efforts to liven the space with framed photographs and a hand-lettered sign that read "Control Room A."

"Where are we now?" Destiny asked, though her tone suggested curiosity rather than her earlier weariness. Their journey had transformed them all, replacing apprehension with anticipation.

Maya examined their surroundings, noting the mid-century fixtures and décor. Their clothing had changed again—slim-fitting dresses in bright colors, with Maya's box

braids styled into an elegant updo. Destiny wore a fashionable shift dress with a geometric pattern, while Kendra's
outfit featured a stylish jacket over a simple sheath dress.

"Judging by the clothes, I'd say early to mid-1960s," Maya
observed. "But I don't immediately recognize—"

She was interrupted by a sound that stopped her
mid-sentence—the most glorious harmony of voices coming from behind a nearby door. Four male voices blending
in perfect unity, backed by a tight rhythm section, creating a
sound so infectious it made standing still nearly impossible.

Destiny's eyes widened. "Is that...?"

"Motown," Kendra breathed, her face lighting up. "We're
at Motown Records."

"Hitsville U.S.A.," Maya confirmed as understanding
dawned. She pointed to a plaque beside the door. "Detroit,
Michigan. The recording studio where Berry Gordy created
the Motown sound and changed American music forever."

The door opened, and a young Black man in a
sharply-tailored suit emerged, flipping through musical notation. He nearly collided with them before looking up in
surprise.

"Oh! Sorry about that," he said, examining them curiously. "Are you with the new girl group Mr. Gordy's auditioning? I thought that was next week."

"No, we're..." Maya began, then hesitated. What exactly were they in this context?

"We're observers," Kendra supplied smoothly, finding confidence in the explanation they'd used throughout their journey. "Here to learn about the recording process. For a school project."

The man's eyebrows rose slightly, but he nodded. "Educational purposes, huh? Well, you should have visitor badges, but..." He glanced at his watch. "We're recording something special today. If you're quiet and stay out of the way, I guess you can observe for a bit." He extended his hand. "Smokey Robinson."

Destiny made a small choking sound, which she quickly disguised as a cough. Maya couldn't blame her—Smokey Robinson, legendary singer-songwriter and Motown executive, looking impossibly young and vibrant, was casually introducing himself as if he wasn't music royalty.

"Thank you, Mr. Robinson," Maya managed, shaking his hand. "We really appreciate it."

"Just Smokey," he corrected with an easy smile. "Mr. Robinson is my father." He gestured toward the door he'd exited. "That's Studio A. The Temptations are laying down tracks for their new record. Behind that door," he pointed further down the hall, "The Supremes are rehearsing for their session this afternoon."

"The Supremes?" Destiny repeated, her voice rising an octave. "As in Diana Ross and The Supremes?"

Smokey gave her an appraising look. "You a fan? They're really starting to take off. That 'Where Did Our Love Go' record is climbing the charts fast."

Maya did a quick mental calculation. If "Where Did Our Love Go" was still climbing the charts, that placed them in the summer of 1964—the beginning of what would later be called "The Motown Invasion."

"We're big fans," Kendra said, managing to sound more composed than Maya felt. "Of all the Motown artists."

"Well, stick around then," Smokey said with a wink. "This place is magical today. Something in the air." He checked his watch again. "I've got to get these charts to the string section. Remember—quiet and out of the way, okay? Berry doesn't like distractions during recording."

With that, he continued down the hall, leaving the three girls staring after him in stunned silence.

"Did that just happen?" Destiny asked finally. "Did Smokey Robinson—THE Smokey Robinson—just casually tell us we could watch The Temptations recording? And mention that The Supremes are literally in the next room?"

"It happened," Maya confirmed, still processing it herself. "We're at Motown Records in 1964, at the exact moment the label is revolutionizing American popular music."

"Not just music," Kendra added thoughtfully. "Culture. Race relations. The Motown artists were crossing over to white audiences in unprecedented ways, breaking barriers on television and radio."

"Berry Gordy's grand vision," Maya agreed. "Creating music with enough soul to appeal to Black audiences but polished enough for white America to embrace."

Destiny was already moving toward the studio door, her earlier fatigue completely forgotten. "Well, what are we waiting for? We have Smokey Robinson's permission to witness music history! Let's go!"

Maya and Kendra exchanged amused glances, following their enthusiastic friend. After the heaviness of witnessing

Greenwood on the eve of its destruction, the prospect of experiencing Motown in its prime was a welcome shift—a chance to celebrate Black excellence that had endured rather than been erased.

They eased the studio door open as quietly as possible, slipping into a small anteroom separated from the main recording area by a large window. Behind a control panel filled with switches, dials, and meters sat two men—one Black, one white—both focused intently on the scene beyond the glass.

And what a scene it was. Five young men in matching suits, standing in a semicircle before microphones, moving in synchronized steps even as they recorded. The Temptations in their prime, voices blending in harmonic perfection as they laid down tracks for what would become one of their signature hits.

The sound was incredible—rich, layered, and vibrant in a way that recordings could never fully capture. Each voice distinct yet merging into a unified whole, backed by Motown's legendary house band, the Funk Brothers.

Maya recognized the song even in its unfinished state: "My Girl," written by Smokey Robinson, soon to become one of Motown's most enduring classics. Hearing it being created—hearing the musicians work through sections, the producer suggesting adjustments, the singers refining their harmonies—was like watching a masterpiece being painted stroke by stroke.

"This is unreal," Destiny whispered, swaying slightly to the music. "We're literally watching them record 'My Girl.' The actual 'My Girl' that's going to be played at weddings and proms for the next sixty years."

"And there's David Ruffin on lead vocals," Kendra noted, pointing to the center figure. "This is his breakout performance with the group."

The recording session continued, the musicians and vocalists working through the song section by section, building it piece by piece with painstaking attention to detail. The process was far more meticulous than Maya had imagined—multiple takes of the same few bars, subtle adjustments to timing and emphasis, the producer occasionally stopping everything to confer with the band.

"I had no idea it was so technical," Destiny observed. "In my head, they just stood around a microphone and sang perfectly the first time."

"Motown was known for its perfectionism," Maya explained. "Berry Gordy ran it almost like a factory—he called it 'The Motown Machine.' Everything was polished until it shined."

After about twenty minutes, the producer called for a break. As the musicians relaxed, one of the Temptations noticed the three girls observing and gestured to his bandmates. They conferred briefly, then one separated from the group and approached the control room.

"New talent?" he asked the producers, nodding toward the girls.

The engineer turned, noticing them for the first time. "Educational observers," he said with a shrug. "Smokey let them in."

The Temptation—Paul Williams, Maya realized—smiled broadly. "Well, educational observers, what do you think of our little song?"

"It's amazing," Destiny gushed, momentarily abandoning her usual cool demeanor. "The harmonies, the arrangement—it's perfect."

"Perfect?" Williams laughed. "We've been at it three hours and still haven't finished. Berry wants it 'just so' before we move on."

"The attention to detail is impressive," Kendra said. "You can hear how intentional every note is."

Williams beamed with pride. "That's the Motown way. Excellence in everything. No cutting corners." He studied them curiously. "You girls sing? You've got the look for it."

"Oh no," Maya said quickly. "We're just... appreciating."

"Everyone sings at Hitsville," Williams insisted good-naturedly. "It's practically a rule. Even the janitors have pipes."

Before they could protest further, he opened the door separating the control room from the studio and waved them in. "Come on, educational observers. Let's see what you've got."

The other Temptations looked up with interest as Williams led the somewhat reluctant girls into the studio. The space felt hallowed somehow—these very floorboards had supported countless musical legends as they created songs that would define American culture.

"Paul, what are you doing?" David Ruffin asked, adjusting his distinctive thick-framed glasses. "We've got twenty minutes before we need to be back on."

"Just having some fun," Williams replied. "These young ladies are here to learn about the recording process. I figured we could give them the full experience."

The other Temptations exchanged amused glances, then shrugged in acceptance. Musicians were still milling about—the bassist tuning his instrument, the drummer adjusting his kit, the guitarists comparing notes on a chord progression.

"So you really want us to sing?" Kendra asked, looking uncharacteristically nervous. "Here? Now?"

"Just for fun," Williams assured her. "Nothing serious. How about something simple—you know 'My Guy' by Mary Wells? We can back you up."

Before they could respond, the studio door opened again, and three young women entered—each immaculately dressed, with perfectly styled hair and elegant makeup. The Supremes, at the very beginning of their reign as Motown's premier girl group.

"We heard there were visitors," said the one in the center—unmistakably Diana Ross, impossibly young and vibrant. "Smokey mentioned it when he dropped off our arrangements."

Maya could practically feel Destiny vibrating with excitement beside her. For all her attempts at playing it cool throughout their journey, this encounter seemed to overwhelm even her practiced nonchalance.

"These young ladies are here for educational purposes," Williams explained. "I was just about to give them a little Motown experience—have them sing with us."

Diana Ross smiled, revealing the famous gap between her front teeth. "Well, don't let us interrupt. We're just waiting for Studio B to free up." She and the other Supremes—Florence Ballard and Mary Wilson—took seats along the wall, an unexpected audience for what was quickly becoming a surreal scenario.

"Oh my God," Destiny whispered to Maya. "The actual Supremes are going to watch us make fools of ourselves. This is simultaneously the best and worst moment of my life."

"We don't have to—" Maya began, but was interrupted by the drummer counting off, followed by the unmistakable intro to "My Guy."

What could they do? They sang.

Kendra, usually the quietest of the three, surprised everyone by taking the lead, her clear voice finding the melody with unexpected confidence. Maya and Destiny jumped in on backup, creating passable harmonies despite their lack of professional training. The Temptations added subtle backing vocals, while the Funk Brothers provided the instrumental magic that made even amateur singers sound good.

It wasn't perfect—they fumbled some lyrics, missed some cues—but the spirit of the moment carried them through. By the chorus, even The Supremes were swaying along, smiling encouragement.

When they finished, everyone in the studio applauded—politely rather than enthusiastically, but still, they had just been applauded by The Temptations and The Supremes. Nothing in their lives, before or after this journey, would quite compare to that.

"Not bad at all," Williams said generously. "You've got potential."

"I like your harmonies," Diana Ross added. "You blend well together. Friends for a long time?"

"Feels like forever," Destiny replied with a sideways glance at her companions.

"That's the secret," Florence Ballard said, her voice rich and warm. "The best groups are friends first, performers second. The audience can feel that connection."

Before the conversation could continue, a man with a clipboard entered the studio. "Break's over, gentlemen. And ladies," he added, noticing The Supremes. "Miss Ross, Mr.

Gordy wants to see you about the Ed Sullivan arrangements before your session."

"Duty calls," Diana said, rising gracefully. "Keep singing, girls. That's how all of us started—just singing anywhere and everywhere until the right person heard us."

As The Supremes departed and The Temptations resumed their positions, Williams directed the girls back to the control room. "Thanks for being good sports," he said with a genuine smile. "Maybe we'll hear you on the radio someday."

"I doubt that," Maya laughed. "But thank you for the experience. It was... unforgettable."

Back in the control room, they watched as the session resumed, the musicians and vocalists picking up exactly where they'd left off, professional focus returning after the brief moment of levity.

"Did that actually just happen?" Destiny asked, her voice hushed with residual awe. "Did we seriously just sing with The Temptations while The Supremes watched? Is that a real thing that occurred in our lives?"

"It happened," Kendra confirmed, looking as stunned as Destiny felt.

"I think this is why the book brought us here," Maya said thoughtfully. "Not just to witness Motown's musical revolution, but to experience joy. To participate in Black excellence, not just observe it."

After the heaviness of their previous jumps—the violence, the resistance, the struggles—this moment of pure creative celebration felt like a gift. Here, in this small studio in Detroit, Black artists weren't fighting for basic rights or defending themselves against violence. They were simply creating beauty, making art so undeniably perfect that America had no choice but to listen.

"It's about more than music," Kendra observed, watching as the producer guided The Temptations through another take. "Motown was creating a cultural bridge in the middle of the Civil Rights era. These songs were playing in white suburbs and Black neighborhoods alike. People who wouldn't sit next to each other on a bus were dancing to the same records."

"Berry Gordy called it 'The Sound of Young America'—not Black America or White America, just America," Maya added. "It was revolutionary in its own way."

"And profitable," Destiny noted pragmatically. "These artists are making serious money, owning businesses, building wealth. Creating an empire with nothing but talent and determination."

They spent the next hour watching the remainder of the session, absorbing the meticulous craftsmanship that went into creating what would become an iconic song. Every take, every adjustment, every decision refined the music until it achieved that distinctive Motown perfection—sophisticated yet accessible, emotional yet polished.

When the session finally concluded, the producer called everyone together to listen to the playback. The energy in the room was electric as the final version filled the studio—that unforgettable intro, the precise rhythm section, David Ruffin's soulful lead vocal, and those perfect harmonies lifting the whole song skyward.

"That's it," the producer declared with satisfaction. "That's the one."

The musicians and vocalists celebrated with handshakes and back-slaps, knowing they'd created something special, though perhaps not realizing just how enduring their work would prove to be.

"If only they knew," Destiny said softly. "This song will still be playing sixty years from now. People not even born yet will dance to it at their weddings."

"Maybe they do know, on some level," Kendra suggested. "You can hear the permanence in the recording, like they understood they were making something timeless."

As the studio began to empty, the familiar tingling sensation started at the base of Maya's spine. "I think we're moving on," she said, not bothering to hide her disappointment. She could have happily spent days in this creative sanctuary.

"Already?" Destiny protested. "But The Supremes are recording later! And Marvin Gaye might show up! And Stevie Wonder! And—"

"And we've seen what we needed to see," Kendra reminded her gently. "Experienced what we needed to experience."

The tingling intensified, the studio beginning to blur around the edges. As they joined hands, preparing for the transition, Paul Williams happened to glance into the control room. He gave them a final wave and smile, unaware that they were not simply leaving the studio but departing his time entirely.

"Thank you," Maya whispered, though he couldn't hear her through the glass. "For the music. For the joy. For showing us another kind of victory."

Then they were falling again, the sounds of Motown fading into the swirling vortex of time. But something of that experience stayed with them—the melody lingering in their minds, the harmony resonating in their hearts. Among all the historical moments they had witnessed, this celebration of Black artistry and excellence would remain one of the brightest.

And as they tumbled through time toward their next destination, they found themselves humming in unison: "I've got sunshine on a cloudy day..."

Chapter 18

The Librarian's Secret

This time, when the world reformed around them, they found themselves in a familiar setting—Dr. Freeman's bookstore. Not the version from 2025 where their journey had begun, but a different iteration of the space. The shelves were arranged differently, the lighting more subdued, the collection of books smaller but no less carefully curated.

"We're back at Sankofa Books," Maya observed, taking in the details that distinguished this version from the one they knew. "But not our time. Look at the décor."

She was right—the furnishings suggested the late 1970s or early 1980s. A poster on the wall advertised an appearance by author Toni Morrison for her new novel "Tar Baby," dating the scene to around 1981.

Their clothing had changed again—Maya now wore high-waisted jeans and a colorful blouse, her box braids adorned with wooden beads and gold cuffs. Kendra's outfit featured a denim jacket over a simple dress, while Destiny sported fashionable wide-leg pants and a fitted top, her hair styled in a sleek bob that perfectly framed her face.

"Dr. Freeman's shop," Kendra confirmed, running her fingers along the spines of nearby books. "But forty years ago."

"But where is Dr. Freeman?" Destiny asked, glancing around the apparently empty store. "And why are we here? This isn't exactly a major historical moment like everything else we've seen."

As if summoned by her question, a door behind the counter opened, and Dr. Freeman emerged—recognizably herself, yet different. Younger, with fewer silver strands in her dark hair, though she still wore an impressive collection of rings on her fingers. She carried a stack of books, which she set down carefully before noticing her visitors.

"Ah," she said, showing no surprise at their presence. "You've arrived. Right on schedule."

"You were expecting us?" Maya asked.

"Of course." Dr. Freeman gestured for them to approach the counter. "The book always works with precision. When it sends travelers, they arrive exactly when and where they're meant to be."

The girls exchanged glances, processing this casual confirmation that Dr. Freeman knew exactly what was happening to them.

"So you know about our... journey?" Kendra ventured.

"I should hope so," Dr. Freeman replied with a slight smile. "I'm the one who set you on it."

"You?" Destiny's eyebrows shot up. "You did this to us? Sent us bouncing through all these historical moments without warning or explanation?"

Dr. Freeman regarded her calmly. "Would you have believed an explanation if I'd offered one? Would you have willingly embarked on this journey if you'd known what it entailed?"

Destiny opened her mouth to argue, then closed it again, considering. "Probably not," she admitted finally.

"Precisely." Dr. Freeman began organizing the books she'd brought out. "Some journeys can only begin with a push rather than an invitation. But now that you've experienced what the book has to show you, you're ready for some answers."

"We have so many questions," Maya said. "About the book, about you, about why we specifically were chosen for this journey."

"And about time," Kendra added. "We've been traveling for what feels like days, but we started on our day off from school. How does that work? Will we return to the exact moment we left?"

Dr. Freeman considered them thoughtfully. "Let's start with the simplest answers. Yes, when your journey concludes, you'll return to the same day you departed—October 11, 2025. Time functions differently when you travel with the book. What feels like days to you will occupy barely a moment in your original timeline."

"Like in Narnia," Destiny suggested. "Where you can spend years there but return to the exact same moment you left."

"A simplistic but not entirely inaccurate comparison," Dr. Freeman acknowledged. "As for why you three were chosen..." She paused, studying each of them in turn. "You weren't, not specifically. The book responds to genuine curiosity about history, to minds open to understanding beyond textbook facts. You happened to be three such minds who found their way to my shop on the right day."

"So it could have been anyone?" Maya asked, not sure if she was disappointed or relieved.

"Not anyone," Dr. Freeman corrected. "The book is selective. It only reveals its capabilities to those prepared to learn from the journey. It's been waiting in my collection for the right visitors—waiting for decades, in fact."

She gestured around the shop. "This bookstore has existed in some form since 1934, though it's moved locations several times. It's always served as a repository not just of books, but of memory—the documented and undocumented history of our people."

"You've owned it since 1934?" Kendra asked, clearly trying to reconcile the mathematics of such a claim.

Dr. Freeman's expression turned enigmatic. "I said it has existed since then. Ownership is a complicated concept when it comes to preserving history." She tapped her fingers thoughtfully on the counter. "Let's just say that 'Dr. Freeman' is more of a position than a specific person. A custodianship passed down through generations."

"Like a time-traveling librarian secret society?" Destiny suggested, half-joking.

"Something like that," Dr. Freeman replied, with surprising seriousness. "There have always been those who understand that history isn't just a record of the past—it's a living force that shapes the present and future. My role—our role—is to ensure that connection remains vital, especially for young people like yourselves."

Maya considered this revelation, finding it both fantastical and somehow deeply plausible. Throughout their journey, they'd encountered Dr. Freeman in different time periods, always with the same purposeful presence, the same enigmatic knowledge.

"So the book," she said, processing this new information. "It's been sending people through time for... how long?"

"Centuries," Dr. Freeman answered simply. "Though it doesn't work for everyone who touches it. It requires a certain... receptiveness."

"And it only shows Black history?" Kendra asked.

"It shows what the reader needs to see," Dr. Freeman corrected. "For you three, that happened to be moments in Black American history—moments connected to your own identities, your own questions, your own future."

"Our future?" Destiny repeated. "What does that mean?"

Dr. Freeman smiled. "That's for you to discover. The journey changes everyone who experiences it, though in different ways. How it changes you will become clear in time."

A question that had been nagging at Maya finally found its voice. "You mentioned the book has been sending travelers for centuries. Have any of them... changed things? Changed history?"

Dr. Freeman's expression turned serious. "An astute question. The answer is both yes and no. The book doesn't allow travelers to alter major historical events—you've discovered that in your own attempts, I believe. But small interactions, personal connections, moments of bearing witness—these can have ripple effects that shape individual lives and decisions."

She reached beneath the counter and produced a familiar leather-bound volume—"The Unwritten History." Placing it carefully on the counter between them, she continued, "History isn't a fixed sequence of events carved in stone. It's a complex tapestry of countless individual choices, actions, and reactions. The book allows travelers to become threads in that tapestry, woven into the larger pattern in subtle but meaningful ways."

"So we might have already changed things without re-alizing it?" Kendra asked. "Just by being present in those moments?"

"Perhaps," Dr. Freeman allowed. "Or perhaps you were always meant to be there—part of those historical moments in ways that conventional recorded history never captured."

Maya's mind reeled at the implications. "That's... that's mind-bending."

"Time usually is," Dr. Freeman agreed with a slight smile. "The important question isn't how you might have changed history, but how history has changed you."

The three friends exchanged glances, each silently ac-knowledging the truth in those words. They had been transformed by their journey—their perspectives widened, their understanding deepened, their connection to history made visceral and personal in ways no classroom education could provide.

"So why bring us here?" Destiny asked, gesturing around the 1981 version of Sankofa Books. "What are we supposed to see or learn in this time and place?"

"This is a waystation," Dr. Freeman explained. "A pause in your journey for reflection and preparation before your final destination."

"Final destination?" Maya echoed. "So our journey is almost over?"

"Nearly," Dr. Freeman confirmed. "You've witnessed struggles and triumphs, resistance and resilience, tragedy and transcendence. You've seen how progress doesn't move in a straight line but follows a more complex pattern of advance and retreat. You've experienced firsthand the courage of those who fought for justice without knowing if they would succeed."

She tapped the book lightly. "There remains one more moment for you to witness—a culmination of sorts, though history itself never truly culminates. It simply continues, evolving with each generation's contributions."

"Will you tell us where—when—we're going next?" Kendra asked.

Dr. Freeman shook her head. "That would defeat the purpose. The book reveals what you need to experience as you need to experience it. Foreknowledge would only dull the impact."

"Worth a try," Destiny muttered, though without real disappointment.

"While you're here," Dr. Freeman continued, "I thought you might appreciate seeing something." She turned and retrieved a large, leather-bound album from a shelf behind the counter. "This might interest you."

She opened the album to reveal photographs—dozens of them, carefully organized and labeled. To Maya's astonishment, the images showed people and places they had encountered on their journey. Claudette Colvin sitting proudly in a church pew, decades older than when they'd met her. The Greenwood District of Tulsa, rebuilt after the massacre, though never returning to its former glory. The Motown studio, preserved as a historical landmark.

"How..." Maya began, then stopped, unsure what she was even asking.

"As I said, Sankofa Books has existed for a long time," Dr. Freeman replied. "We document more than most people realize."

As they flipped through the album, a particular photograph caught Maya's attention—three teenage girls in 1950s clothing, barely visible at the edge of a crowd gathered to hear Mamie Till-Mobley speak. The image was grainy and distant, but unmistakably them.

"That's us," she whispered, pointing to the photo. "We're in these pictures."

"Of course you are," Dr. Freeman said matter-of-factly. "You were there. History recorded your presence, even if conventional history books didn't."

Kendra turned the page and gasped softly. There they were again, this time standing at the back of the room during the Civil Rights Act signing. And again, watching from the sidewalk as students integrated the University of Alabama. Each historical moment they'd visited had somehow captured their presence, preserving it in these meticulously maintained photographs.

"This is wild," Destiny said, touching one of the images as if to confirm its reality. "We're literally in historical photographs. We're part of the record."

"More than you might realize," Dr. Freeman mused. "History isn't just what's written in textbooks or shown in documentaries. It's the accumulated presence of everyone who participated, everyone who witnessed, everyone who remembered."

She turned to the final page of the album, revealing a blank space with a small notation beneath it: "November 4, 2008."

"What's this?" Maya asked, though a suspicion was already forming in her mind.

"Your next destination," Dr. Freeman replied. "The page awaits your presence to be complete."

November

4, 2008. The date resonated in Maya's mind—an evening she had heard about countless times from her parents, a night of tears and celebration, of history being made in real time.

"We're going to witness Obama's election," she said, certainty filling her voice. "The night America elected its first Black president."

Dr. Freeman neither confirmed nor denied this, simply closing the album. "You've traveled from moments of oppression and resistance to moments of cultural achievement and artistic expression. Your journey has shown you the complexity of progress, the price of change, the courage of ordinary people in extraordinary circumstances. What comes next is for you to experience, not for me to reveal."

The familiar tingling sensation began at the base of Maya's spine, right on cue. "I think it's time," she said to her friends, reaching for their hands. "Our final jump."

"Wait," Destiny said suddenly, turning to Dr. Freeman. "Will we remember all this when we get back to our own time? Or will it fade like a dream?"

Dr. Freeman's expression softened slightly. "That depends on you. Some travelers return with perfect recall, their lives forever altered by what they've witnessed. Others find the memories becoming hazy, more feeling than fact. But none return unchanged, whether they fully remember the details or not."

"I don't want to forget," Kendra said quietly. "Any of it. Even the painful parts."

"Then don't," Dr. Freeman said simply. "The mind preserves what matters most to the heart. If you choose to remember, you will."

The tingling intensified, the bookstore beginning to blur around them. Dr. Freeman remained clear, however, watching them with an expression that suggested both satisfaction and a hint of sadness.

"One last piece of advice," she said as reality began to dissolve. "When you return to your own time, remember that you're not just witnesses to history—you're makers of it. Every choice, every action, every moment of courage or compassion contributes to the ongoing story. Your day off is ending, but your real work is just beginning."

Maya felt those words settle into her soul as the bookstore faded around them. Dr. Freeman—whoever or whatever she truly was—had given them more than a journey through time. She had given them a purpose, a responsibility, a connection to something larger than themselves.

Then they were falling again, three friends linked by clasped hands and shared experiences, tumbling toward their final historical destination—and after that, back to their own time, their own lives, forever transformed by what they had seen and learned on their extraordinary day off.

Chapter 19

Yes We Can

The transition felt different this time—not the usual disorienting tumble through space and time but something smoother, like being carried on a gentle current. When the world solidified around them, they found themselves standing in what appeared to be someone's living room. A modest space filled with mismatched furniture, family photos on the walls, and an atmosphere of excited anticipation.

The room was packed with people of all ages—grandparents in comfortable armchairs, parents perched on sofa arms, children sprawled on a worn carpet. Everyone's attention was fixed on a large television where news anchors discussed exit polls, electoral maps, and projected outcomes.

"November 4, 2008," Maya whispered, recognizing the scene immediately. "Obama versus McCain. Election night."

Their clothing had changed again, modernized to fit the late 2000s—jeans and hoodies for Maya and Kendra, while Destiny sported leggings and an oversized sweater. Maya's box braids were styled simply, and all three wore "VOTE" buttons pinned to their clothes.

"We're at someone's election watch party," Kendra observed, taking in the crowd. At least twenty people had squeezed into the modestly-sized living room, many wearing Obama campaign shirts or buttons.

"But whose party?" Destiny wondered. "And where?"

As if answering her question, a woman emerged from the kitchen carrying a tray of snacks. She was in her early thirties, with a warm smile and tired eyes that suggested long hours of campaign volunteering.

"Girls, can you help bring in the rest of the food?" she called to them, clearly mistaking them for expected guests. "People are getting hungry, and we've still got a long night ahead before they call this thing."

"Sure," Maya replied automatically, never one to refuse a request for help. She nudged her friends toward the kitchen, whispering, "Just go with it."

The kitchen was a hive of activity—more people chopping vegetables, arranging crackers on plates, and mixing punch. Signs of a hastily organized celebration were everywhere: campaign flyers repurposed as placemats, plastic cups with "Obama 2008" written in marker, and a hastily baked sheet cake decorated with red, white, and blue frosting.

"Here," a teenage boy about their age handed Destiny a platter of buffalo wings. "Take these out before my uncle Brian eats them all. He's been stress-eating since they called Kentucky for McCain."

"On it," Destiny said, accepting the platter while eyeing the wings with undisguised interest. "Though I might need to quality-test one first. Food safety and all that."

"Destiny," Kendra hissed, "we're here on a mission, not for snacks."

"Who says we can't do both?" Destiny countered, deftly snagging a wing before carrying the platter into the living room. "Time travel makes me hungry, and I've been through like eight decades today without proper sustenance."

Maya and Kendra followed with their own food trays, marveling at how easily they'd been absorbed into this gathering. No one questioned their presence or asked who had invited them—the collective excitement of the evening had erased normal social boundaries, creating an instant community united by hope and nervous anticipation.

"Pennsylvania goes to Obama!" someone shouted from the living room. A cheer erupted, followed by high-fives and hugs.

They returned to find the mood significantly more optimistic, the tension in the room shifting from anxiety to cautious excitement. On screen, commentators discussed Obama's mounting electoral votes, though they repeatedly emphasized that many key states remained too close to call.

"I forgot how long election night takes," Maya said, settling onto a floor cushion. "My parents told me stories about staying up until like three in the morning waiting for the final call."

"You mean you don't remember who wins?" an elderly man seated nearby asked with a wink. "Seems like something that's hard to forget."

"Oh, I know who wins," Maya assured him, realizing too late how her comment might have sounded. "I just meant the waiting is tough."

"Tell me about it," the man chuckled. "I've been waiting eighty-three years to see a Black man with a real shot at the presidency. A few more hours won't kill me, but they might test my blood pressure."

As the evening progressed, the girls found themselves fully immersed in the experience—cheering when states were called for Obama, groaning when McCain claimed others, sharing the collective emotional rollercoaster of a historic election night.

Destiny, true to form, had befriended half the room within an hour, charming grandmothers and making children laugh with her exaggerated campaign slogans. "Yes we can... eat all these buffalo wings!" she declared, causing a nearby group to erupt in laughter.

"You are incorrigible," Kendra told her, though she couldn't hide her own smile.

"What? I'm channeling the historic nature of the moment through food," Destiny defended herself. "It's a perfectly valid coping mechanism for overwhelming emotions. Plus, these wings are fantastic."

Kendra had settled into a conversation with a group of college students, discussing the grassroots organizing that had characterized Obama's campaign. Her thoughtful observations and questions revealed how much she had grown throughout their journey—no longer the hesitant, uncertain girl who had first touched the book in Dr. Freeman's shop.

"The youth turnout has been unprecedented," one student was saying. "People who never cared about politics before are suddenly engaged."

"Because it feels like there's actually something at stake," Kendra replied. "Something possible that wasn't possible before."

The student nodded enthusiastically. "Exactly! Hope is a powerful motivator."

Maya found herself beside the elderly man who had commented on her earlier remark. His name was Ernest, and he wore his Obama button pinned to a VFW cap that identified him as a Korean War veteran.

"You young folks don't remember what it was like," he was saying, his voice soft with memory. "There was a time when I couldn't even vote, let alone imagine someone who looked like me in the White House."

"When did you cast your first vote?" Maya asked, genuinely interested.

"1952, Eisenhower versus Stevenson. Had to pay a poll tax and pass a 'literacy test' that asked impossible questions about the state constitution." He shook his head at the memory. "They didn't want us voting, made it clear every step of the way. But we persisted."

Maya thought of the Selma marchers they had learned about, of Claudette Colvin and Rosa Parks, of all the people who had sacrificed so much for the right this room full of people now exercised freely.

"Worth it?" she asked softly.

Ernest's eyes, clouded with cataracts but bright with emotion, fixed on the television screen where the electoral map showed Obama steadily gaining ground. "Every bit of it," he said. "Every bit."

A commotion near the television drew everyone's attention. The networks had just called another key state for Obama.

"Ohio goes blue!" someone shouted, triggering the loudest celebration yet. People were jumping up and down, hugging, some wiping away tears. The path to victory was becoming clearer with each update.

"No way McCain comes back from this," the teenage boy who had given Destiny the wings declared confidently. "It's happening. It's really happening."

"Don't jinx it!" his mother scolded, though her own expression betrayed similar excitement.

As the night wore on, the mood in the room continued to shift. What had begun as nervous hope transformed into growing confidence, then barely contained jubilation as Obama's electoral count approached the magic number of 270.

"Look at this," Kendra said, gesturing around the room. "Black, white, young, old—everyone coming together. This is what we've been seeing throughout our journey, isn't it? The long, slow work of building bridges."

"Some longer and slower than others," Destiny agreed, uncharacteristically reflective. "But yeah, this feels like... I don't know, not an ending, but a milestone. Something earned through all those struggles we witnessed."

"It's the power of voting," Maya added, thinking of Ernest's story. "All those people who fought for that right knew exactly what they were doing—creating the tools for change that would outlive them."

"Speaking of tools for change," Destiny said, abruptly shifting back to her typical tone, "I'm going to revolutionize this veggie platter situation. Who puts cauliflower next to ranch dip but puts the carrots across the table? Criminal design, honestly." She stood and headed toward the snack table, clearly on a mission of platter reorganization.

Maya and Kendra exchanged amused glances, grateful for Destiny's knack for lightening even the most profound moments.

"She hasn't changed a bit," Kendra observed.

"I'm not so sure," Maya replied, watching as Destiny paused to help an elderly woman find a napkin. "She's still Destiny, but I think she's seeing things differently now. We all are."

Suddenly, a hush fell over the room. On screen, the news anchor's expression had turned solemn.

"CNN is now prepared to make a major projection," he announced. "With the polls closed and the results counted in key battleground states, we can now project that Senator Barack Obama will become the 44th President of the United States."

For one suspended moment, the room was absolutely silent, as if everyone needed a heartbeat to absorb the magnitude of what they'd just heard. Then the silence exploded into chaos—people leaping to their feet, screaming, crying, hugging anyone within reach. Someone turned up the volume as the cameras cut to Grant Park in Chicago, where thousands had gathered to await the results.

The three friends found themselves swept into the celebration, passed from embrace to embrace by people who were now crying openly, expressions of joy and disbelief mingling on their faces.

"We did it! We actually did it!" the woman who had first mistaken them for helpers kept repeating, mascara streaming down her cheeks.

Ernest, the elderly veteran, sat perfectly still in his chair, tears flowing unchecked down his weathered face. "I never thought I'd live to see this day," he said to no one in particular. "My grandaddy was a slave, and now a Black man is president."

The television showed crowds celebrating across America—in Harlem, in Atlanta, in Detroit, in cities and towns everywhere. People flooding into streets, embracing strangers, waving American flags with a renewed sense of possibility.

"Look at their faces," Maya said to her friends as they huddled together in a corner, watching the scene unfold both in the living room and on television. "This is joy. This is hope made visible."

"It's like everything we've been seeing throughout our journey led to this moment," Kendra observed. "Not as an endpoint, but as proof that progress, however slow and difficult, is possible."

"And look who's making it happen," Destiny added, gesturing to the diverse crowd both in the living room and on the screen. "Not just Black people, but a coalition. Everyone who believed change was possible."

"You know what this reminds me of?" Maya said suddenly. "All those moments in history when people took action without knowing if it would ever lead to success. Claudette Colvin had no idea when she refused to give up her seat that we'd eventually see this day. The NASA mathematicians couldn't have imagined a Black president when they were calculating rocket trajectories in segregated offices."

"They had faith without proof," Kendra agreed. "They pushed forward because it was right, not because victory was guaranteed."

"And some of them lived to see this moment," Destiny added. "Like Ernest over there. Imagine what this feels like for him."

On television, President-elect Obama appeared on stage in Grant Park, his family beside him, his posture both triumphant and humbled by the historic weight of the moment. The crowd in the living room fell quiet again, gathering around the television to hear his victory speech.

"That's going to be the most-watched speech in history," someone nearby commented. "Every word will be analyzed for generations."

As Obama began to speak—that familiar cadence, that measured optimism—Maya felt herself transported back through all the historical moments they had witnessed. She could almost see the thread connecting Claudette Colvin to the NASA mathematicians to the Motown artists breaking cultural barriers to this culminating moment of possibility.

"If there is anyone out there who still doubts that America is a place where all things are possible," Obama said, his voice carrying clearly through the room, "who still wonders if the dream of our founders is alive in our time, who still questions the power of our democracy, tonight is your answer."

The crowd in Grant Park erupted, the emotion so palpable it seemed to vibrate through the television screen. In the living room, people were wiping away tears, nodding in solemn agreement, some simply standing in stunned silence at the reality of what they were witnessing.

"I wonder if we should try to find Dr. Freeman," Kendra whispered to Maya. "She said this was our final destination. Maybe she's here somewhere."

Maya scanned the room but saw no sign of their enigmatic guide. "I don't think she needs to be physically present," she replied. "She knew we'd understand the significance of this moment on our own."

"This victory alone is not the change we seek," Obama was saying. "It is only the chance for us to make that change. And that cannot happen if we go back to the way things were. It cannot happen without you, without a new spirit of service, a new spirit of sacrifice."

Those words seemed directed specifically at them, an echo of Dr. Freeman's parting message: "You're not just witnesses to history—you're makers of it."

"I think I'm starting to understand what this whole journey was about," Maya said quietly.

"What?" Destiny asked, rejoining them with a plate improbably piled high with desserts. "Besides giving me an excuse to sample food across the decades?"

"It's about connection," Maya replied, ignoring Destiny's snack obsession with practiced ease. "Connecting us to our history in a way that makes it real, not just facts in textbooks. Making us understand viscerally what people sacrificed, what they built, what they dreamed of."

"So we'd be motivated to continue the work," Kendra added, the realization dawning in her eyes. "Because progress isn't guaranteed. It has to be earned by each generation."

"Heavy responsibility for a day off," Destiny commented around a mouthful of cake. "But I get it. Hard to go back to being self-absorbed teenagers after seeing what we've seen."

"You? Self-absorbed?" Kendra teased. "I'm shocked."

"Hey, I contain multitudes," Destiny defended herself. "I can care about fashion AND justice. Style AND substance. Cake AND social progress."

Maya laughed, feeling a lightness she hadn't expected in this moment. They had witnessed so much pain, so much struggle throughout their journey—yet here they were, laughing together while watching the culmination of centuries of work for equality. Perhaps that too was part of the lesson: that joy and humor remained essential elements of resilience and progress.

As Obama's speech reached its emotional peak, with his repeated refrain of "Yes we can," Maya noticed something strange happening. The NCNW pin she'd been wearing throughout their jumps began to warm against her collar, glowing faintly in the dimly lit room.

"Guys," she whispered, touching the pin. "Something's happening."

Kendra and Destiny checked their own pins, finding them similarly warm and luminous.

"Is this... is this the book calling us back?" Destiny asked, her expression caught between excitement and reluctance. "Are we going home?"

Before anyone could answer, Maya noticed something even stranger. In the corner of the room, barely visible in the shadows, stood a familiar figure—Dr. Freeman, watching them with unmistakable satisfaction. She raised a hand in acknowledgment, then pressed a finger to her lips in a gesture of silence before fading into the darkness.

"Did you see—?" Maya began.

"Dr. Freeman," Kendra nodded. "She's here."

"So what now?" Destiny asked, glancing at her glowing pin with nervous anticipation. "Do we just... go walk over to her? Wait for the speech to end? Finish this excellent cake first?" She held up her plate defensively.

"I think," Maya said, watching as Obama concluded his address to thunderous applause, "we're meant to experience this moment fully before we move on. This is what Dr. Freeman called a 'culmination'—not an ending, but a milestone on a continuing journey."

As the speech concluded and the celebration in the living room resumed with renewed energy, the three friends remained huddled in their corner, each lost in their own thoughts yet connected by their shared experience.

"If we do go back soon," Kendra said after a moment, "I want to remember everything. Every person we met, every moment we witnessed. I'm going to draw it all when we get home—create a record of everything we saw."

"And I'm going to read everything I can find about the people and places we visited," Maya added. "Fill in the gaps, learn the details we missed."

"And I," Destiny declared, setting down her now-empty plate, "am going to start a fashion line inspired by every era we visited. 'The Claudette Collection' featuring subtle rebel vibes beneath respectable exteriors. 'Motown Glamour' with modern twists. 'Greenwood Entrepreneurial Chic' celebrating Black business excellence."

"Of course you are," Kendra laughed. "Turning historical revelation into fashion innovation."

"Hey, we all process in our own ways," Destiny defended herself with dignity. "Some sketch, some study, some design. It's all valid."

Maya felt a surge of affection for her friends, for their unique perspectives and personalities that had remained fundamentally themselves throughout their extraordinary journey. They had seen so much, learned so much, yet remained Maya, Kendra, and Destiny—just with expanded horizons and deeper understanding.

As the celebration continued around them, Maya noticed the glow from their pins intensifying slightly. She felt no tingling sensation yet, but sensed that their time in this historical moment was drawing to a close.

"I think we should find Dr. Freeman," she suggested. "I have a feeling she's waiting for us."

"One more thing first," Destiny said. She grabbed three plastic cups from a nearby table, filled them with sparkling cider, and handed them to her friends. "A toast. To history—not just witnessing it, but being part of it."

"To understanding where we've been," Kendra added, raising her cup.

"And to shaping where we're going," Maya finished.

They clinked their cups together just as the pins' glow brightened dramatically, enveloping them in a gentle radiance that went unnoticed by the celebrating crowd. The world around them began to fade slightly at the edges, not with the usual disorienting spin but with a gentle dissolving, as if they were being called rather than pulled away.

"I think this is it," Kendra whispered. "Our last jump."

"Back to 2025?" Destiny asked. "Back to our regular lives after all this?"

"Not regular anymore," Maya replied, feeling the transition beginning in earnest now. "Not after everything we've seen."

As the election night celebration began to blur around them, Maya caught one last glimpse of Ernest, the elderly veteran. He was smiling now, his weathered face transformed by joy, the fulfillment of hopes he had carried for a lifetime visible in his eyes. It was an image she knew she would carry with her always—the living embodiment of history's long arc, bending at last toward justice.

Then the scene faded completely, and they were moving once more through time and space, the warm glow of their pins guiding them forward—or perhaps backward—toward whatever awaited them next.

Chapter 20
Back to the Future

The transition back to their own time wasn't what Maya had expected. No disorienting tumble through space, no dizzying kaleidoscope of colors and sounds. Instead, it felt more like stepping through a doorway—one moment they were surrounded by the jubilant celebration of Obama's election victory, and the next they were standing exactly where their journey had begun: in Sankofa Books, 2025, in front of the shelf where Maya had first discovered "The Unwritten History."

For a moment, they simply stared at each other in stunned silence, as if confirming that all three had actually returned together. They were back in their original clothes—Maya in her button-down and jeans, Kendra in her paint-splattered overalls, Destiny in her vintage jacket.

The NCNW pins they'd received at the Civil Rights Act signing were still attached to their collars, the only physical evidence of their extraordinary journey.

"Well," Destiny finally said, breaking the silence, "that was the weirdest Black Girls Day Off activity ever. Ten out of ten, would not recommend for the faint of heart, but the snacks throughout history were surprisingly decent."

"Did that really just happen?" Kendra asked, her voice hushed with awe. "Did we actually time-travel through pivotal moments in Black history, or did we collectively hallucinate after touching a weird book?"

Maya glanced at the shelf where she'd found the book, but "The Unwritten History" was no longer there. In its place sat a slim volume titled "Remembering Forward: The Cyclical Nature of Progress," its author listed as Dr. E. Freeman.

"It happened," she said with certainty. "All of it."

"But how long were we gone?" Kendra wondered, checking her phone. "According to this, it's still October 11th. Only twenty minutes have passed since we entered the store."

"Dr. Freeman said we'd return to the same day," Maya reminded them. "Time works differently when you travel with the book."

"So my mom won't kill me for disappearing for what felt like weeks," Destiny said, visibly relieved. "That's the first good news I've heard all century. Literally."

Maya snorted at the unexpected time pun, the tension of their return breaking as all three dissolved into slightly hysterical laughter. They had witnessed some of history's most profound and painful moments, and here they were, giggling like the teenagers they still were, despite everything they'd experienced.

"I can't believe we sang backup for The Temptations," Destiny said when she could speak again, wiping tears of laughter from her eyes. "Like, that actually happened. Diana Ross witnessed my pitchy alto."

"And we saw Obama elected," Kendra added, her expression sobering slightly. "We were there for that moment, Maya. We saw what it meant to people like Ernest."

"We saw so much," Maya agreed. "Claudette Colvin's arrest. Greenwood before the massacre. The NASA mathematicians. Moments that changed everything."

"And now we're just... back," Destiny said, looking around the bookstore with new eyes. "Expected to go on with normal teenage life after witnessing pivotal moments in American history. That seems unfair, to be honest."

"Speaking of the store," Kendra said, "where's Dr. Freeman? Shouldn't she be here? This is her place, after all."

As if summoned by her name, Dr. Freeman emerged from behind a shelf, carrying a stack of books. She looked exactly as she had when they'd first met her—elegant, composed, those distinctive silver rings adorning her fingers. Nothing in her demeanor suggested she'd just orchestrated an extraordinary journey through time.

"Finding everything you need?" she asked casually, as if they'd simply been browsing books for the past twenty minutes instead of traveling through decades of history.

The three girls stared at her in disbelief.

"Are you serious right now?" Destiny finally sputtered. "Finding everything we need? We just toured Black history's greatest hits, both tragic and triumphant, and you're acting like we've been comparing book prices?"

Dr. Freeman's lips curved in a slight smile. "And how was your journey? Illuminating, I hope?"

"Illuminating doesn't begin to cover it," Maya said. "We saw... everything. Claudette Colvin's arrest. Mamie Till-Mobley's courage. The Motown recording studio. The NASA mathematicians. Greenwood before it was destroyed. Obama's election night."

"And don't forget the buffalo wings in 2008," Destiny added. "Historically significant buffalo wings."

Dr. Freeman nodded, seemingly satisfied with their account. "The book shows what you need to see. For each traveler, the journey is different."

"But why us?" Kendra asked, the question that had lingered throughout their adventure. "Out of all the people who must visit this store, why were we chosen for this experience?"

"The book responds to genuine curiosity and open hearts," Dr. Freeman replied, shelving the books she'd been carrying. "You three possess both. And perhaps it sensed that you would carry what you learned forward in meaningful ways."

"No pressure or anything," Destiny muttered. "Just casually carry forward the weight of Black historical knowledge like it's a cute tote bag and not an existential responsibility."

"Does this happen often?" Maya asked, gesturing toward the space where the book had been. "People accidentally time-traveling from your bookstore?"

"More often than you might think," Dr. Freeman replied enigmatically. "Though not everyone experiences it as fully as you three did. Some glimpse only fragments, moments. Others resist the journey entirely and simply see an ordinary book."

"So what now?" Kendra asked. "We just... go back to our regular lives? After everything we've seen?"

Dr. Freeman studied them thoughtfully. "What do you think you should do with the understanding you've gained?"

The three friends exchanged glances, each considering the question.

"I'm going to read everything I can find about the people and places we visited," Maya said after a moment. "Especially the stories that don't make it into mainstream history books. The Claudette Colvins overshadowed by the Rosa Parks. The Greenwoods erased by violence. The hidden figures behind the headlines."

"I'm going to draw it all," Kendra added with new-found conviction. "Create visual records of what we witnessed—not just the events themselves, but how it felt to be there. The emotions behind the historical facts."

"And I," Destiny declared grandly, "am going to create the most historically informed, socially conscious fashion line the world has ever seen. 'The Claudette Collection' for subtle rebels. 'Hidden Figures Workwear' for brilliant minds. 'Greenwood Entrepreneurial Chic' celebrating Black business excellence."

"Of course you are," Kendra laughed. "Turning historical revelation into fashion innovation."

"Don't hate," Destiny replied with dignity. "Fashion is political. You think those perfectly pressed suits and dresses the Freedom Riders wore were just about looking cute? That was armor. Respectability as both shield and weapon."

Maya blinked in surprise at this unexpectedly profound observation. "That's... actually really insightful, Destiny."

"I contain multitudes," Destiny shrugged. "Just because I care about looking good doesn't mean I can't also care about justice. Style AND substance, baby."

Dr. Freeman watched this exchange with evident approval. "You see?" she said. "Each of you will process what you've learned in your own way. That's exactly as it should be."

She moved to the counter and retrieved something from beneath it—three small journal books, each with a different colored cover. "For recording your experiences," she explained, handing one to each of them. "Memory is fallible, even for events as extraordinary as what you've witnessed."

Maya accepted the burgundy journal, tracing her fingers over its leather cover. "Thank you," she said sincerely. "For everything. Even if your methods were a bit... unconventional."

"Would you have believed me if I'd simply told you what the book could do?" Dr. Freeman asked with a knowing smile. "Would you have willingly embarked on such a journey?"

"Hard no," Destiny replied immediately. "If someone had said 'Hey, want to witness various traumatic moments in Black history, including violent racism, while also getting to see some cool cultural achievements?' I would have suggested a movie instead. Much less running involved."

Dr. Freeman chuckled. "And yet, having experienced it, would you trade the knowledge you've gained?"

Destiny considered this, then sighed in defeat. "No," she admitted. "Even with the terror and the uncomfortable period clothing and the lack of decent hair products throughout most of American history... no, I wouldn't trade it."

"Me neither," Kendra agreed softly.

"Nor I," Maya added.

Dr. Freeman nodded, satisfied with their answers. "Then the book chose well." She glanced at her watch. "And now, perhaps, you should continue your day off? I believe you had other plans before your unexpected historical detour."

"Waffles," Destiny gasped, as if suddenly remembering a long-lost love. "We were going to get waffles. I haven't had proper food in what feels like days."

"You literally ate buffalo wings in 2008," Kendra pointed out.

"That was historically significant stress-eating, not proper nutrition," Destiny countered. "Plus, I need to process everything we just experienced, and my brain works better with syrup."

Maya laughed, feeling a wave of affection for her ridiculous, wonderful friend. Despite everything they'd witnessed—the trauma, the triumph, the profound historical moments—Destiny remained fundamentally Destiny, and there was something deeply comforting in that constancy.

"Waffles it is," she agreed, tucking her new journal into her backpack. "And then maybe we can start mapping out everything we saw? Create a timeline of our journey?"

"Only you would suggest homework on our day off," Destiny groaned, though her expression was fond rather than truly exasperated. "Fine. Waffles first, historical documentation second. But I'm going to need at least a triple order to fuel this academic endeavor."

As they prepared to leave the bookstore, Maya paused, turning back to Dr. Freeman. "Will we ever see you again? Or the book?"

"The book finds those who need it," Dr. Freeman replied with her characteristic enigmatic smile. "And as for me... Sankofa Books isn't going anywhere. Neither am I."

"Cryptic as ever," Destiny muttered. "Would it kill you to give a straight answer just once?"

"Possibly," Dr. Freeman said, her expression suddenly mischievous. "Historical knowledge suggests direct answers often lead to decreased narrative tension and reduced character development."

Destiny's mouth fell open in shock. "Did you just make a joke? About narrative structure? After sending us tumbling through time and space?"

"I contain multitudes," Dr. Freeman replied, echoing Destiny's earlier words with a serene smile.

Maya couldn't help laughing at Destiny's outraged expression. "Come on," she said, pulling her friend toward the door. "Waffles await, and I think we've had enough mind-bending revelations for one day."

As they stepped outside into the bright October sunshine, the ordinary world of 2025 Orlando continued around them as if nothing had changed—though they certainly had. People walked by on their way to work or school, completely unaware that three teenage girls emerging from this unassuming bookstore had just returned from the most extraordinary history lesson imaginable.

"It's weird," Kendra said as they walked down the street. "Everything looks exactly the same, but it all feels different somehow."

"Because we're seeing it with new context," Maya suggested. "Understanding where it all came from, what it cost to get here."

"And how fragile progress can be," Destiny added, her tone uncharacteristically serious. "How easily things can slide backward if people stop pushing forward."

"That's what Dr. Freeman meant," Kendra realized. "About us not just being witnesses to history, but makers of it. Every generation has to do the work."

"Deep thoughts before waffles," Destiny complained, though her expression remained thoughtful. "Can we please focus on maple syrup and whipped cream before we tackle ongoing historical responsibility?"

"Priorities," Maya laughed, linking arms with both her friends as they headed toward the waffle house.

"Absolutely," Destiny agreed. "Waffles, then revolution. In that order."

As they walked, Maya found herself seeing their familiar neighborhood with new eyes—noticing which businesses were Black-owned, which buildings had historical significance, which street names honored figures from the past. Their journey had given her a heightened awareness of how history shaped the present, how the struggles and triumphs they had witnessed had created the world they moved through every day.

"Hey," Kendra said suddenly, "do you think we were always meant to take this journey? Like, was October 11th always going to be the day we accidentally time-traveled through Black history instead of just getting waffles?"

"That's getting into some serious metaphysical territory," Maya replied. "Free will versus determinism. Causality paradoxes. The nature of time itself."

"Or maybe," Destiny suggested, "we just happened to touch a weird magical book on our day off, and now we're overthinking everything because we haven't eaten proper waffles yet."

"Also possible," Maya conceded with a smile.

When they reached the waffle house—a small, Black-owned restaurant that had been their original destination before all the historical detours—they slid into a booth near the window. The menu was exactly as Maya remembered, the prices blessedly reasonable, the smells of cooking batter and brewing coffee filling the air with ordinary comfort.

"So," she said as they studied their menus, "what was everyone's favorite historical moment? Besides the buffalo wings," she added quickly, cutting off Destiny's inevitable answer.

"Honestly? Motown," Destiny admitted. "Hearing 'My Girl' being recorded, singing with The Temptations, getting feedback from actual Diana Ross? That was beyond incredible."

"I loved the NASA mathematicians," Kendra said. "Seeing those brilliant women doing such complex work in such restrictive circumstances. The quiet determination of it all."

"For me, it was Obama's election night," Maya decided. "Seeing how everything we'd witnessed throughout our journey led to that moment. The threads connecting Claudette Colvin to the voting rights marchers to Ernest watching the first Black president get elected."

"Speaking of threads," Destiny said, reaching into her jacket pocket. "Look what I found."

She pulled out a small piece of fabric—blue with a white geometric pattern. It took Maya a moment to recognize it.

"Is that from Greenwood?" she asked, amazed. "From the fabric store we visited?"

Destiny nodded. "I picked it up while we were there. Must have been in my pocket when we jumped. And look—" She reached into her other pocket and produced a Motown recording studio visitor badge. "Souvenirs from our excellent adventure."

"I thought we couldn't bring things back!" Kendra exclaimed, checking her own pockets hopefully.

"Apparently we can," Maya said, remembering the NCNW pins still attached to their collars. "Maybe because they're small? Or maybe because the book allowed it?"

"Or maybe because I have extremely good taste in historical memorabilia," Destiny suggested, tucking the fabric sample carefully back into her pocket. "Future fashion inspiration, right here."

Their waitress arrived to take their order, bemused by Destiny's request for "one of everything with a side of historical perspective," which she eventually translated to a giant breakfast sampler with extra whipped cream.

As they waited for their food, Kendra pulled out her phone and opened the photo gallery. "I wonder..." she murmured, scrolling through recent images.

"What are you looking for?" Maya asked.

"I tried to take pictures," Kendra admitted sheepishly. "During our jumps. When you guys weren't looking."

"You what?" Maya exclaimed. "But our phones didn't even work in the past!"

"I know, but I had to try," Kendra defended herself. "Think about it - photographic evidence of historical moments no one else has ever captured! The Motown recording session, Greenwood before the massacre, the NASA mathematicians at work..."

"Did you seriously try to become a historical paparazzi without telling us?" Destiny asked, looking both impressed and scandalized. "That's actually brilliant. Totally useless since the phones didn't work, but brilliant."

Kendra's shoulders slumped as she continued scrolling. "Yeah, well, it was worth a shot. But there's nothing here. Not a single photo saved."

"Of course not," Maya said, though she couldn't help feeling a pang of disappointment. "That would be too easy. Too concrete."

"I guess we just have to rely on our memories," Kendra said, putting her phone away. "And my sketches, once I recreate them."

"And my fabric sample," Destiny added, patting her pocket where the small piece of Greenwood textile was safely stored. "Some souvenirs made it back, at least."

Maya's phone buzzed with a text from her mom, checking in on their day off activities. She stared at the screen, suddenly struck by the absurdity of their situation. How could she possibly convey what they'd experienced in a casual text message?

"What should I tell her?" she asked her friends, showing them the message. "Having waffles after time-traveling through pivotal moments in Black history. NBD."

"Just say we're learning important historical lessons while supporting a Black-owned business," Kendra suggested pragmatically.

"Which is technically true," Destiny pointed out through a mouthful of waffle. "Just minus the whole 'we were actually there' part."

Maya typed a quick response, then set her phone aside. There would be time later to try to explain—or not explain—what had happened to them today. For now, she wanted to be present in this moment, with her friends, processing the extraordinary journey they had shared.

"You know what's funny?" she said as they continued eating. "We set out this morning wanting to celebrate Black Girls Day Off by connecting with our culture and history. And that's exactly what we did—just in the most literal way possible."

"Be careful what you wish for," Kendra laughed. "You might end up singing with Motown legends."

"Or running from slave catchers," Destiny added soberly, then brightened. "But also eating buffalo wings with the first Black president's election team, so it balances out."

"I don't think that's how it works," Maya said, though she couldn't help smiling.

"It is now," Destiny declared. "That's my historical interpretation, and I'm sticking to it."

As they finished their waffles and paid the bill (leaving an extra-generous tip, as Destiny insisted historical awareness should translate to economic justice), Maya felt a strange mixture of emotions—the lingering awe of what they'd experienced, alongside the comforting ordinariness of being three friends sharing a meal on their day off from school.

Outside the restaurant, they paused, suddenly uncertain about how to proceed with the remainder of their day. After witnessing pivotal moments in Black history, a trip to the mall seemed almost comically trivial.

"So," Kendra said, "what now? Movie? Shopping? More historical research?"

"Honestly?" Destiny replied, stretching luxuriously in the October sunshine. "I vote for the mall. After all that heavy historical significance, I need some mindless consumerism to balance my chakras or whatever."

"The mall?" Maya repeated, surprised. "Really? After everything we've seen?"

"Especially after everything we've seen," Destiny insisted. "Look, we just witnessed decades of struggle and triumph, pain and progress. We carried the emotional weight of centuries in a single day. I think we've earned the right to look at overpriced sneakers and pretend to be normal teenagers for a few hours."

"She has a point," Kendra conceded. "We can't live in historical significance mode all the time. Even activists need breaks."

Maya considered this, then nodded slowly. "Mall it is. But," she added with a smile, "I'm bringing my new journal. When inspiration strikes about our journey, I want to capture it."

"And I'm definitely sketching people at the food court," Kendra decided. "Practicing for my historical series."

"And I'll be critically analyzing current fashion trends through a historical lens," Destiny declared grandly. "While also buying whatever's cute and on sale."

They set off toward the bus stop, three ordinary-seeming teenage girls on a day off from school, carrying an extraordinary secret. As they walked, Maya found herself noticing details she might have missed before—the names of streets commemorating historical figures, businesses owned by descendants of the Great Migration, cultural touchstones that connected their present to the past they had witnessed firsthand.

"You know what?" she said suddenly. "I think I get why it's called 'Sankofa' now."

"The bookstore?" Kendra asked.

"It's more than just a name," Maya explained. "Sankofa is a concept from Ghana. It's represented by a bird looking backward, with an egg in its mouth. It means 'go back and get it'—the idea that we have to reach back into the past to understand who we are and move forward properly."

"So that's what Dr. Freeman was doing," Destiny realized. "Sending us back to 'get' our history, to bring it forward with us."

"Exactly," Maya nodded. "We literally went back to get it."

"Well," Destiny said, linking arms with her friends as they reached the bus stop, "mission accomplished, I'd say. Though next time, I'm bringing better shoes and modern hair products."

"Next time?" Kendra echoed, alarmed. "You think there's going to be a next time?"

"With our luck?" Destiny grinned. "Absolutely. But hopefully not until after the mall. A girl has priorities."

As the bus arrived and they climbed aboard, Maya found herself smiling at her friends' banter. They had witnessed some of history's most profound moments, carried the weight of their people's struggles and triumphs across time, and emerged changed but still fundamentally themselves—Maya, Kendra, and Destiny, three friends on a day off that had become so much more.

Outside the bus window, Orlando rolled by—a city shaped by all the forces they had witnessed, a present built upon the past they had experienced firsthand. And somewhere in that city, in an unassuming bookstore with an ancient secret, Dr. Freeman was probably shelving books, waiting for the next curious minds to discover what history had to teach them.

But for now, they had waffles in their stomachs, mall adventures ahead, and the shared understanding that while their Black Girls Day Off might be drawing to a close, their journey with what they had learned was just beginning.

"So," Destiny asked as the bus rumbled toward the mall, "what should we do for next year's Black Girls Day Off? Because I've got ideas that would blow your mind."

Maya and Kendra exchanged alarmed glances, then dissolved into laughter that drew curious looks from other passengers.

"Maybe something with less time travel?" Kendra suggested.

"And fewer life-threatening historical moments?" Maya added.

"Fine," Destiny sighed dramatically. "Regular history museum tour it is. But I'm bringing snacks. Historically accurate ones, of course."

Some things, it seemed, would never change—and that, Maya decided, was exactly as it should be.

Author's Note

I first discovered Black Girls Day Off while scrolling through social media one evening—a hashtag, a movement, a declaration of communal joy and rest that immediately captured my attention. As someone who came to the United States from the Caribbean, I was struck by this intentional celebration of Black womanhood and the radical act of claiming time for oneself in a world that rarely encourages Black girls to pause.

When I began writing this novel, I thought I was crafting a simple story about three teenagers taking a day off from school. But like Maya, Kendra, and Destiny, I found myself on an unexpected journey—one that took me deep into the rich, complex tapestry of African American history that I hadn't fully understood before making my home here.

Growing up in the Caribbean, my understanding of Blackness existed in a different context. I knew my own island's history, our struggles for independence, our cultural traditions. But the specific contours of the African American experience—the Great Migration, the Green Book, Black Wall Street, the hidden NASA mathematicians—these were histories I encountered only after arriving in the United States. And like the girls in this story, I found myself both heartbroken by the painful chapters and uplifted by the extraordinary resilience.

I won't pretend this learning curve has been easy. Since moving here, I've experienced painful moments of racism that took me by surprise—interactions that reminded me that despite shared ancestry, my Caribbean background had not prepared me for the particular way race functions in American society. There were days when, like Destiny confronting the destruction of Greenwood, I wanted to look away from these harsh realities.

But alongside these difficulties, I've discovered the incomparable joy of African American culture—the music, the literature, the food, the humor, the unbreakable spirit that transforms struggle into art, resistance into celebration, memory into fuel for forward movement. I've found community in unexpected places, shared understanding across different Black experiences, and a sense of belonging within this broader diaspora.

This novel evolved from a simple concept into something much more personal: my own journey of Sankofa—reaching back to understand history in order to move forward with greater purpose. Through researching each historical moment the girls encounter, I found myself developing a deeper appreciation for the ground I now stand on and the shoulders I stand upon.

Like Maya, Kendra, and Destiny returning from their time-traveling adventure, I emerge from writing this book changed but still myself—carrying new understanding while maintaining my Caribbean identity, bearing witness to painful truths while celebrating the joy that has always been central to Black survival.

My hope is that readers of all backgrounds might see themselves in these three girls—in Maya's thoughtful curiosity, Kendra's quiet observation, Destiny's irrepressible spirit—and join them in discovering how the past shapes our present and how understanding history can transform how we move through the world.

After all, we are all time travelers in our own way, carrying ancestral memories forward, building bridges between what was and what could be. And sometimes, the most meaningful journeys happen on days that begin with nothing more ambitious than waffles with friends.

Thank you for joining Maya, Kendra, Destiny, and me on this unexpected adventure through time, history, and identity. May it inspire your own journey of discovery, wherever you may be from and wherever you may be going.

With gratitude,

Leah T. Williams

Also by

Leah T. Williams

So, you made it to the end of *Black Girls Day Off*. Thanks for reading. But if you think that means you're done here, think again. There are more stories waiting for you—different places, different characters, but all with the same pull that brought you to the end of this one.

What to Read Next

Neither Out Far Nor In Deep – A Caribbean coming-of-age story full of family, friendships, and choices that hit harder than a wayward coconut. If you've ever wanted to feel like you were standing on an island, soaking in the sun and drama, this one's for you.

Where Is Noemi – A young adult mystery that will make you question how well you really know the people closest to you. If you're the type to read a book and try to solve the mystery before the main character does, go ahead and test your skills.

Sweet Like Sugar Cane – The *prequel* to *Neither Out Far Nor In Deep*, because mango doesn't fall far from the tree. Some love stories don't just fade away. Some stick with you, shape you, refuse to let go. Readers kept asking about *that* love story. Now you finally get to see how it all started.

Where the Guava Tree Stands – A novel-in-verse about family, legacy, and figuring out who you are when everything feels like it's pulling you in different directions. It's poetry, but with a story that grabs you and won't let go.

Stay Connected

If you liked this book, I've got plenty more where that came from.

Instagram, Facebook, TikTok: @kittiwriter1
Website: www.leahtwilliams.net

And if you *really* liked it, leave a review. It helps more than you think—and it lets me know people are actually reading these books instead of just stacking them on their shelves for decoration.

www.ingramcontent.com/pod-product-compliance
Lightning Source LLC
Chambersburg PA
CBHW071231300726
48975CB00002B/374